ROUNI
JUNIPER VALLEY

Red carried on with the roping while I talked and gentled down the mustangs that had learned to face the rope quietly. We managed to have twenty-eight good horses broke to the rope by nightfall.

"I wish we could water 'em," Red said as darkness

PRAISE FOR
THE WESTERNS OF JACK CURTIS

WILD RIVER MASSACRE

"Plenty of gunsmoke and hot lead to satisfy most . . . aficionados of the genre."

—Si Brandner, *The Capital Journal* (Pierre, SD)

BLOOD TO BURN

"Worth every penny."

—Eli Setencich, *Fresno Bee*

PARADISE VALLEY

"Memorable images sparkle."

—*Books of the Southwest*

THE JURY ON SMOKY HILL

"The best Jack Curtis book so far, with plenty of mystery and suspense."

—Wayne Barton, coauthor of
Manhunt and *Live by the Gun*

"A story line as old as the West but as refreshing and new as the spring air and flowers of April and May. Curtis makes it easy for us to lean back and relax and enjoy an hour or so away from our daily cares. We are treated to an exciting, suspenseful drama. Run, don't walk, to the nearest bookstore and purchase this book."

—Don Warren, *Western Review*

BLOOD CUT

"A book for all 'old west' fans. The author takes you back in time to when men were men and you knew who the good guys were. He also makes you feel that you are there as he characterizes his characters in such a believable manner. . . . Make this a must on your list."

—Don Warren, *Western Review*

TEXAS RULES

"Original. . . . a good powder burner that will leave readers satisfied that Western writers, though using a familiar form, still possess the ability to provide a new wrinkle for an old story."

—Lawrence Clayton, *Abilene Reporter-News*

"Dynamic, action-packed. . . . Curtis pushes all the right buttons, just as he did in *Blood Cut*. . . . This book is even better than *Blood Cut* and I thought that it was the best new Western novel that I had read in a long time. . . . Cotton Dunbar is a strong character, and if John Wayne were alive and this was made into a movie he would be ideal for the role."

—Don Warren, *Western Reivew*

THE SHERIFF KILL

"Fine Western adventure featuring a complex antagonist. Heartily recommended."

—*Booklist*

Books by Jack Curtis

JACK CURTIS
THE QUIET COWBOY

POCKET BOOKS

New York   London   Toronto   Sydney   Tokyo   Singapore

This book is a work of fiction. Names, characters, places, and incidents are products of the author's imagination or are used fictitiously. Any resemblance to actual events or locales or persons, living or dead, is entirely coincidental.

An *Original* Publication of POCKET BOOKS

POCKET BOOKS, a division of Simon & Schuster Inc.
1230 Avenue of the Americas, New York, NY 10020

Copyright © 1994 by the Curtis Family Trust

ISBN: 0-671-79317-9

First Pocket Books printing October 1994

10 9 8 7 6 5 4 3 2 1

POCKET and colophon are registered trademarks of Simon & Schuster Inc.

Cover art by Garin Baker

Printed in the U.S.A.

THE QUIET COWBOY

— 1 —

G OT YOUR LIST?" I ASKED, WATCHING THE HIND END OF
the buckskin out of habit as I fitted my boot into the box
stirrup and swung up. He was a gentle gelding, but it's a
cautionary habit that pays off, especially on chilly mornings when any horse feels some fractious.

Red patted his breast pocket and nodded. He was
already aboard his big blue Appaloosa and waiting. "You
got the money?" he asked without smiling, even though I
knew it was his kind of Indian joke, teasing me for trying
to plan things out to save time.

Red had a long, fuzzy Paiute name that probably
sounded as good as Tom or Bill to them, but to the whites
it came out like Fresh Bear Shit in the Woods, so
someone had named him Red a long time ago and he
never complained.

Sometimes he called me Nez, which I know means
nose in voyageur French, but in Paiute it probably means
Fresh Coyote Pee on the Fence Post.

He was built like his Appy, big in the shoulder with a

short-coupled torso round as a rain barrel, and close to the ground with thick legs that left no slack in his jeans.

He wore his hair in a braided club that drooped down from the back of his big hat, and he had a face that looked small compared to the size of his head, as if someone had taken a walnut burl and carved a thin little mouth, a bird bill of a nose, and close-set eyes in the middle of it.

With that kind of a little face set into a larger bulging head, it's hard to ever see a smile or any kind of an emotion. You have to go by the sound of the voice or what his eyes are doing.

"Your gun?"

"In my saddlebag," he said.

It was his way. He didn't like to wear the gun because he had to cinch the belt so tight around his middle, which was the same circumference as his hips and his chest.

Wearing the gun belt was a precautionary habit for me, and I generally felt more comfortable with it, even though the chances of using it between the ranch and Buttonwillow were near zero. It all weighed, including the Colt Frontier and thirty .44-caliber cartridges in the loops, something like six pounds.

We figured it had to be the first Saturday in July from the almanac Wolf Aufdemburg gave us last January, although we'd argued about it because it seemed more like Monday to me.

Red claimed it was Saturday because he'd marked each day off with his pencil. He kept it hanging in the outhouse, where he meditated every morning after breakfast.

"Maybe you got bound up in the middle of June," I argued.

"No." He shook his head. "I'm as regular as an eight-day clock."

"How come?"

"Prune cake."

We argued some more, but he had the book and all I

had was my feeling it was Monday, which was worth about as much as a catfish on a sandbank.

Wasn't any sense fighting about it. We'd tried that one time when we were cabin-bound by a freak blizzard. We'd got at it over whether the color of a horse affected his good sense. Red claimed all black horses were smarter than any other color.

"It's a fact," he'd concluded, shuffling the deck of faded cards for the millionth time with a ripping sound.

"Prove it," I'd said, setting my pen and paper in a safe place.

"I ain't lyin'," he'd said.

"You're full of bullshit," I said.

"Anybody knows anything about horses knows blacks are smarter," he'd come back sharply.

I guess it was we both needed a physical workout to get rid of the cabin poison that had accumulated all during January, and this was one way of doing it.

"You're sayin' now I don't know horses after I been dealin' in horses since before you were ropin' goats?"

He threw the cards in my face for that, and I hit him on the side of his round head, and then it became a pretty interestin' kind of a fracas where we managed to break the table and the packing box chairs, knock the stovepipe down, which filled up the place with smoke, and do some damage to each other, too.

Hittin' him was like hittin' an old black oak stump, and though I managed to bark his skin, I never once budged his head off his shoulders, and when I got tired hittin' him and my fists were killin' me, he started his own punches at right about my belly button and moved up like he was goin' up a ladder until he was gettin' through my pawin' left, landing some fair head shots that would have made a Spanish mule proud.

The damn smoke from the stove choked us down and I went to the floor to get some air and he followed a moment later, then we both crawled out the door into the snow.

3

After a while when he'd got his wind back, he looked at my hands, and spit some blood from a cut in his mouth. "You got weak hands," he said, gripping the dislocated thumb of my left hand, pulling it out and working it back in place.

When he started working on the pushed-back knuckles on my right hand, I studied his closing left eye, and the gash in his iron eyebrow where no doubt I'd broken my hand.

"Better bandage that one tight for a while," he said.

After that we kept busy patchin' up the furniture and putting the tin stovepipe back up and cleaning the blood out of the place.

The first Saturday in February we went into Buttonwillow for supplies as always, with the bandages gone and the cuts and bruises pretty much healed.

No one in town said anything about it although Marvin Bohn, the saloon keeper, had let his eyes dwell a half second extra on my face so I was set to ruin my hand again on his bald head he kept hidden under a derby.

"Glad to see you're wintering so well, Wes," he said, and I let it pass.

Now with the sun and the long days, that little house-keeping upset was more like a hibernating dream that neither one of us wanted to repeat.

We'd even made a kind of a pledge that we'd set up the ranch next fall so there'd be just a few animals and they would be turned back on the range to look after themselves while we rode south into old Mexico until we found folks that didn't know what a sheepskin coat was.

This chilly morning, we didn't push our horses along the trail half growed over with sagebrush and creosote bush that ran northeast toward Buttonwillow. There wasn't anything in that town to hurry for. You could see it inside out in about the time it takes to water a mule.

Our spread on the western edge of the Juniper Valley was in my name because I'd had enough cash to give Mex Abrams, the banker, the down payment, but I wouldn't have tried it without a first-class horse peeler like Red for a partner.

It was something like fifteen miles into town and we let our horses take their time warming up, looking at the scant forage on the open range, seeing a few pronghorn antelope feeding nervously in the distance, and watching the hawks and buzzards sailing across the pale blue sky cluttered with a few slow-time clouds. The only tracks on the trail were made by wild horses and stray cattle. Hardly anyone ever came out this far for a visit.

Beecher Turnbull had come out with Dee Gibbon and Luis Huerta, a couple of his half-assed gunhands, a few months before when the mesquite grass was coming up strong. He'd started spouting off that any animals on his range were his, and I answered that mavericks on public land—whether they were mustangs or longhorns—belonged to the man who put his brand on them.

"Maverickers on my range have uncommon bad luck," Turnbull had said from his lofty perch aboard a long-legged chestnut thoroughbred.

"I haven't been east of Buttonwillow since I took up this place," I told him, "but if I figure I've got some stray stock over that way on public domain, I'll go after them."

Everyone knew that once or twice a year some foot-loose cowboy would disappear and maybe turn up on Turnbull's so-called range pretty well chopped up by buzzards and coyotes. That type of person never seems to have a family or close friends, so there wasn't anyone to complain about it, and Turnbull had let it be known that strangers riding in his general area might find it risky.

The county sheriff, way to hell and gone over at Ponca Sink, pretended he never heard about it. There wasn't anything he could do anyway, because it was always a case of long-range dry-gulching where you couldn't prove anything.

But Beecher Turnbull didn't mind riding around in broad daylight with a long-barreled .44 Springfield or a

.38-55 Winchester in his rifle boot instead of the short-barreled saddle gun most riders carried.

Folks made some guesses but they wrote it off as part of the wild country. It's too damned hard of a life catching mustangs, breaking them to ride, then finding a buyer, without having to put up with ornery cusses like Turnbull.

It don't make a rider feel too cheery thinking somebody's back yonder all set to blow your backbone through your brisket. A man out in the lonesome can get to brooding and ruin his appetite.

"If you're done, you can go," I'd said to Turnbull, trying not to provoke a gunfight over nothing.

Red had them covered from the window in the cabin and Turnbull knew it.

"What I said goes for that dumb injun, too," he said loudly, as he turned the chestnut thoroughbred and led his two hardcases down the trail toward town.

Seeing his broad back swaying in rhythm with the thoroughbred's gait, I couldn't help thinking about Jean Louise, the girl he'd married, kind of a tomboy school-marm I might could have been fond of.

They'd put on a box social at the school, and I'd bid on a supper that I figured was hers because it was tied with the same kind of red ribbon on the wrapping that she used to tie up her bright whiskey-colored ponytail with.

Once I bid, I was afraid it would turn out to be Thelma Parker's or Metta Snapp's, but I didn't need to worry because Beecher Turnbull got into the bidding and he had enough money to buy anything he wanted.

Later on after supper when the fiddler started playing slow songs, Jean Louise come over and said, "Would you care to dance with me, Wesley?"

"Shucks, I wouldn't know waltzin' from tryin' rasslin' holts," I stuttered.

The fiddles started playing "I Dream of Jeanie with the Light Brown Hair," and she waltzed me around so I never felt so good.

I remember she looked up at me with her honest blue eyes and said, *"I sure appreciate knowin' you, Wesley."*

'Course I didn't know what to say, so I croaked and swallowed my tongue, and when the dance was over, I had to hand her back to Beecher Turnbull.

Turnbull was our last visitor, if you didn't count Babe Silliman, the sewing machine salesman who was always driving his special-made light spring wagon all over the territory selling Grover and Baker machines, carrying the news, and in some magic manner sidlin' up alongside the womenfolk in such a way that he stayed in the territory even though most all of them had already bought a machine.

There was another traveling man, a roader named Ace Dietjen, who drove a buckboard with a string of plugs tied on behind, buying, selling, and trading. Mostly it was trading, with him getting a little extra money to boot.

With us it was different. Ace came out to our place because once in a while we'd have a horse with a born fault he could fix for an hour or two or a blemish he could cover up, and we'd set a fair price which he usually paid, although always with the familiar complaint that a workingman couldn't make any money off horses anymore. We took it as a kind of worn-out joke on us, because he was the one making the money and we were the ones doing the work.

As we rode along, we passed an occasional side track that would lead off to an abandoned ranch where someone in a wet year had found a water hole and tried to make something of it, but the country was too dependent on winter rains that usually were cut off by the Sierras. If you didn't catch the rainy year to start with, you were likely going to have to suffer a couple of dry ones that would smarten you up and send you on over the mountains.

Sometimes we used these old abandoned ranches if their corrals were still strong enough to hold a band of wild horses, and sometimes we'd camp near the water hole, but never in the dusty windblown cabins, because there'd always be a rat family living in there, and a rattlesnake family sharing the quarters.

The wild horses could stand the dry country better than humans, although it was hard going and they'd be gaunted down to ribs and thin guts. Maybe they'd drift on north if there was no feed at all, and of course a certain number would die.

It was this wrinkle that made Beecher Turnbull think he owned the wild horses wherever they were, because it was his custom to take his big Springfield out to the horse herds, find a shady high spot where he could rest that long rifle on a rock, and shoot all the studs that weren't cut and branded, which left more feed for the others. Then he'd take out a blooded stallion to breed the wild mares and let nature work for him.

He figured that gave him more rights than anyone else to the wild horses in the whole broad valley even though his spread was close to thirty miles east of ours, clear on the other side of Buttonwillow.

The snow we'd had in January had helped bring up a good stand of cedillo grass and there was plenty of it left even though it had turned brown and you'd think it would be without much nourishment, but the hot summer sun had cured it quickly, and the horses still relished it.

"That old grass is goin' to send us to the palm trees of Mexico," I said as we rode along. It made me feel good to know that things were going right for us, and we had a good chance to lay back in a hammock by a big, wet river and listen to the señoritas sing.

"They make pie down there?" Red asked.

"If they don't, you can teach 'em."

"I don't want to do anything." Red shook his head. "I just want some pie and cookies and cake and custard pudding."

"That's asking for quite a speck."

"I bet they sprinkle sugar on tortillas and fry 'em."

"No. They're a civilized people." I pretended I knew something about the subject. "They make all those fancy European pastries, you know."

"No. I don't know."

"Well, it's like they make a sweet biscuit, then they cut a hole in it and stuff it with plum jam, then they cover it up with melted chocolate and put raisins and nuts all over the top."

"God, I can't wait," Red murmured, smacking his lips, his little features inside his big head squinching up in silent joy.

"First we have to catch another bunch of broncs and gentle them down."

"Maybe they'll show me how to do that . . ."

"Do what?"

"Drip that melted chocolate all over."

"I'd rather you put your mind on mustangs."

"There's a good band over in Prayer Valley," he muttered.

"Red, that's mighty close to halfway to Turnbull's."

"They ain't his," Red said stubbornly. "Maybe he's got an old Tee-Bar stud in there, but the mares are wild and the colts ain't been branded."

"We'll start Monday," I said.

Coming along the track, dust puffing up from the horses' hooves, we rode along in silence for a while, attending to the larks on the rise, the occasional limber-legged jackrabbits leaping and veering from fear of nothing, the condition of ranging cattle, saddles creaking in the quiet, my buckskin's shoulders working under my hand, until we cut into the main east-west old stage road that made a curve because of a rocky hill on around into town.

On the bluff on the outskirts stood the famous two-story, white-painted gingerbreaded house with its high cupolas, verandas, balconies, and the widow's walk on top.

Compared to anything else in Buttonwillow it was a

magnificent structure, and would have been completely out of place except if you knew that it had been built by Beecher Turnbull when he married Jean Louise, pretending it was a gift from him to her.

Anyone could look at the big, tall house sitting on the bluff with the lookout on top of it and figure that the man who built it wanted to stand up there and look around in every direction and say, "Mine, all mine."

In a way, Turnbull had built the house for his bride, because being an educated lady, she would have wasted away at his ranch headquarters built way out on the flats where the wind blew powdered alkali across every afternoon and made everyone red-eyed and grumpy. The headquarters was only three miles from Buttonwillow and the way the Tee-Bar was growing, the big two-story house would be in the center of Turnbull's empire soon enough.

"Much house," Red commented as we rode by.

I had nothing to add to it. We'd already said what we thought it looked like and what it might mean. Being as we weren't too far from Turnbull's ranch, we noticed how the smaller spreads in Juniper Valley seemed to be falling into his hands, and the way the town's businesses that survived were all renting Mex Abrams's buildings.

"Reckon Turnbull will swaller Abrams, or the other way?" I asked.

"You lookin' for a bet?" Red answered.

"No. It's too close. Abrams is smarter, but Turnbull's bigger."

"I wouldn't give a dime's worth of dog meat for the whole shebang," Red said carelessly. "If I was goin' to swallow up a country, I'd pick somethin' besides high desert."

"Maybe he don't know any different," I said.

"He was born somewhere different," Red said stubbornly. "Nobody was born here. The only mystery is why they come here and stayed."

"You're here," I said, seeing the first town buildings on down the slope.

"But only so long as the mustangs are free for the gathering."

"Then where?"

"¿Quien sabe?" he shrugged, uncaring.

The two-block main street of Buttonwillow looked as it did every Saturday. A few buckboards and ranch wagons were drawn up near the mercantile or the blacksmith shop. Some horses stood at the hitch rail, mostly all cactus-welted, nondescript hammerheads that didn't show much in the way of good looks but were, nonetheless, powerful little brutes with amazing endurance.

The lucky ones had copper crickets on their bits that they could play with and roll with their tongues to pass the hours.

At the far end of the street was the Glad Tidings Church, which had missed a coat of paint some years back and now was scoured by sand and dried out by the sun.

On the back corner was Dad Crawford's livery stable and corral, which naturally was in worse shape than the church.

Wayne Farnhorst's harness shop had a little door cut into a big wide door so a person could come and go without causing much of a fuss or, when Farnhorst needed to fit a double set of four-in-hand harnesses, he could open the big door and bring the horses inside.

Marshal Witherspoon's office and jail stood next to the harness shop, and next to that was the mercantile owned by Wolf Aufdemburg. Across the street was Jacob Levy's haberdashery, Tuck Krendel's barbershop, and the Prince Albert saloon.

On down the next block was a ladies' goods store, Ed's Cafe, Wade Filson's blacksmith shop, and Frank Pedragal's drayage, which was mainly a corral with a storage shed. Then there was the schoolhouse and E.

Mickelsen "Mex" Abrams's bank on the corner, Edna Lewis's rooming house, and offices for Tom Meredith, the combination vet, doc, oculist, dentist, and waterdowser, and Bolivar Cromwell, the lawyer. Back of the alleys were small houses where the townsfolk lived with their families.

There were a few other shacks and yards on down the hill where the old, worked-out derelicts scraped by on the leavings of others. Old Dag Petersen, Widow Parker, Van Winger, who was an old mountain man and a war veteran down with rheumatism, and that just about was the whole of it, except for the Mexicans and Indians and one old black man called Nigger Joe. They were the fartherest down the slope, where about every ten years a flash flood would clean off their shacks and trash.

We tied up in front of the Mercantile. It was a big plain building with a wide entryway built two steps up from the boardwalk which made a comfortable place for the old ones to set and watch the world go by.

Red slipped the canvas saddlebags off the Appy's big butt and we walked past gray-haired Van Winger sitting on the front step carving on a soft pine ball inside another ball, making a scattering of splinters and curls on his lap and long, dirty beard. I noticed the padding he'd sewed onto the knees of his pants with waxed string, and figured his knees were getting so bad he was crawling more than he was walking now.

Helluva note for a pioneer and army scout to end up crawling from his shack up to the mercantile steps just so he wouldn't feel so god-awful alone.

We said hello as we went on inside, and right away the smell of dry goods hit us, along with the lesser perfumes of arnica and cheese and new boots. The scents of spices and dill pickles, of salt herring, coal oil, brooms, and patent medicines, of hard candy and shaving soap, of gunpowder, tobacco, and lard, sulfur, and cinnamon bark, of turpentine and oats, coffee, and pickled salmon mingled together into a perfume so particularly belonging to that business that if you put it in a bottle you'd have to name it General Store.

Wolf Aufdemburg was at the fartherest-back counter weighing out pink beans from a gunnysack into two-pound paper bags. His hands were small and pink, without a callus, rope burn, scar, or finger warped from a misset break. To me they looked like overgrown baby hands, and something about the way he handled the wooden scoop brought up the salt in me.

His face was equally bland and unblemished, except for small-lensed eyeglasses that perched on the bridge of his nose well below heavy, furry eyebrows that twisted up at the ends. His pale skin set off the bright pink in his fat cheeks and then there was nothing but fine fair hair that was growing gray at about the same speed that it was disappearing. He was the man with a perpetual smile and quick, evasive eyes.

Looking up at me over the gold rims of his glasses, he said, "Hellow, Wesley. It must be the first Saturday of the month."

"I reckon," I said. "Can you fill out Red's list and add on a new two-blade jackknife?"

Red handed over the list, and the storekeeper read it slowly and half aloud to make sure he could read Red's writing.

"Cinnamon, mace, loaf sugar, fine sugar, cloves, dried currants, sultana raisins, butter, eggs, baking powder, molasses, brandy, vanilla extract, almond extract—no, I don't got dat one—coriander, ginger, orange peel—no, out here? You crazy?—baking soda, okay, cream of tartar, coconut—Coconut! Vere you gettin' these ideas?"

"From Mrs. Cole's cookbook," Red replied, daring the kraut to make a joke.

"Ya, okay, vat else? Beans, side of bacon, cornmeal, lard, buckwheat meal—anything else?"

"My jackknife," I reminded him. "A Barlow."

"And make it orange extract if you don't have orange peel," Red said.

"Okay. I'll get it ready," he said, taking the canvas paniers. "No viskey?"

"We just drink in public," I said and started to turn back toward the door.

"Hear the town's growin'," Aufdemburg cackled as if he'd made a joke.

"How's that?"

"Beecher Turnbull brought his kid brother out from back east."

Aufdemburg seemed to think there was something juicy to relish in that, but it meant nothing to me and I didn't follow it up.

We were on our way out when the team bells jingled on the door and in came Jean Louise carrying a small parasol.

Young, but with a mature bearing, Jean Louise Turnbull wore a simple belted gingham dress that neither hid nor emphasized her slim waist and high bosom, and over her strong shoulders she wore a pale blue lace shawl that reflected the blue of her eyes. I liked the way she'd used a red silk ribbon to gather her whiskey-colored hair into a frisky ponytail that hung carelessly down her back as if she were poking fun at all the staid mannerisms people load themselves down with. Like a flag of freedom, that gathered fall was a protest against wound-up-tight braids and buns, and also a nervy poke in Old Time's melancholy ribs.

She noticed me and Red, looked me square in the eye, and without changing her smile said warmly, "Hello, Wesley," and passed on down the aisle toward the dry goods section, where Wolf Aufdemburg was bobbing his fat head up and down, wiping his sweaty hands nervously on his denim apron, saying, "Good afternoon, Mrs. Turnbull, good afternoon . . . good afternoon, ma'am . . ."

"What do you want to do now?" I asked Red when we

were outside, being polite because I knew what he'd say, and thinking how direct and honest her eyes were.

"You want to see what kind of pie they got over at Ed's?"

"What'll you bet they don't have apple?" I kidded him.

"I hope it's something besides apple. I can make an apple pie anytime."

For a fact he could and did. So long as the dried apples would hold out, we never were short on apple pie out at the cabin.

Once in a while, whenever he'd overdo it, I'd start singin' that old stage driver's song:

> The farmer takes the gnarliest fruit,
> Wormy, bitter, and hard, to boot.
> They leave the hulls to make us cough
> And don't take half the peelings off.
> Then on a dirty cord they're strung
> And from some privy window hung
> And there they serve as a roost for flies
> Until they're ready to make pies.
> Tread on my toes or tell me lies,
> But please don't make any more apple pies . . .

That would usually switch him over to molasses pecan pie or dried peach cobbler.

Ed hollered a greeting to us as we came in the small restaurant, then with a laugh yelled into the kitchen, "Two slabs of cherry pie, Melba!"

"And coffee," Red added, holding back any expression of joy at finding his favorite dessert.

Ed stumped along back into the kitchen on his peg leg, and brought out the coffee and pie.

With Ed watching, Red took a bite, nodded, swallowed, and said, "Butter crust. Good."

"It's all right, Melba, you can come out now," Ed laughed and hooted. "Red says you won the blue ribbon."

"He knows better'n to say anything else," she yelled back. "Now don't bother me no more, I got spuds to mash."

"She's afraid to come out because she's blushing with pride," Ed said in a low voice, glancing over his shoulder. "She figured you boys'd be in today and fixed the pie special."

"You tell her I'm goin' to dream about this pie," Red said.

"I'd marry it if it could wash clothes," I said.

"You hear the news about Beech Turnbull?" Ed said, acting like Wolf Aufdemburg sharing his gossip.

"No," I said.

"His kid brother's here."

I liked Ed enough to ask. "So?"

"There'll be trouble," Ed said carefully.

"Why?" Red asked.

"Beech ain't travelin' like a colt no more, and Jean Louise, well, she's not even twenty-one yet . . ." He nodded his head wisely. "'Course I wouldn't want to wish any hard luck on anybody as well liked as Beech"— he winked one eye as he talked—"but that combination looks promising."

"Likely," I said, laying out some change, not wanting to get into that kind of grimy chatter where nobody wins and nothing comes out right.

We stood by the hitch rail a while, letting our digestion work, minding our own business, when Marshal Witherspoon came slouching along, a toothpick between his big horse teeth, and with a kind of a leisurely pace that ordinary cowboys don't have. Cowboys know they can't walk far and hate to walk at all, so when they do have to, they make it fast, barely short of a trot.

Marshal Witherspoon, not a big man, but lean and erect, always had a look on his face that seemed to say, "You're guilty." At least it did to me, and I hadn't been much outside the law since leaving Arizona in a hurry.

I sometimes wondered if he couldn't toll in the guilty

ones and make 'em confess just by looking at them that way. He was known to have been a gunman at one time in Nogales, and he wore his six-shooter tied down. He'd been hired when the word got out there was silver in the Reese River country and the rush's overflow had moved into Buttonwillow. Witherspoon had killed one crazy-drunk halfwit and that had ended any more problems with the miners, and as soon as word came in of a rich strike at Mansfield in California, they all left. Those that could, anyway—old Dag Petersen's arthritis had fixed him by then and he was left behind.

Witherspoon's tight cheeks were threaded with purple veins and he smelled of alcohol, but his step was steady and his gray eyes were clear.

After saying hello, he leaned against the polished hitch rail and asked, "How's it out west?"

"Not bad. The grass is holding up, and there's still enough wild ones."

"Heard Beecher Turnbull bought out old man Salkeld?"

"Nothing much there," I said. "It's just a quarter section of sagebrush."

"Has the spring though. Only one in that country."

"True," I said, not needing to go into the argument that because a man owns the water, don't mean he owns everything else, including the wild horses that had been drinking at the same watering hole since the Spaniards lost them up this way a couple hundred years ago.

He was warning me of something that I couldn't figure exactly. For a fact Beecher Turnbull was creeping up on us one water hole at a time, but I didn't see it as dangerous yet.

"They brought in Everett Mabry a couple weeks back. One of the Tee-Bar found his remains out east."

"That'd be Bud Mabry's kin?" I asked.

"Some kind of a nephew or something," the marshal said. "He had a jackknife in his pocket and a short runnin' iron in his boot."

"Dry-gulched?"

"Like the others." He spit out the toothpick, nodded, and walked leisurely on up the boardwalk.

When he was gone, I looked at Red. "Ready to fog on out of this heller of a country?"

"No. Likely somebody'll shoot him before he gets to crowdin' us," Red said.

It was too early to go back home. I didn't feel like settin' still long enough to get my head washed and my hair cut, and there wasn't any sporting women in town except for the Widow Parker, who didn't hardly count because she had to know you and fix up a signal for you to sneak in the back door, then try not to step on her kids sleeping on the floor in the dark, then more or less agree to marry her in the distant future, then leave a gold eagle on the kitchen table and tiptoe out the back door again.

A man had to have an overdeveloped urge in order to overcome all those obstacles to romance, not to mention that she was a spindling little lady who had unfortunately been kicked in the face by a steel-shod horse when she was younger.

Still, we had time to kill and, of the same mind, we wandered across the street to the Prince Albert. We went inside, secretly hoping that maybe, just maybe, a young lady down on her luck might have strayed in there in the hopes of making a few friends.

=== 2 ===

I HAD NOT HOPED TOO MUCH, SO THAT I WASN'T TOO DISAP-
pointed to find that the only thing female in the place was
a big picture hanging over the bar depicting a plump,
rosy-skinned lady lying on a brass bed, eating grapes. She
rested in such a way that I could see one Percheron-sized
haunch, almost one and a half bosoms, and her navel, but
the most interesting parts were obscured by brass rails
and adornments. I always wondered why the artist didn't
move over a couple of feet and do an honest job, and said
so when I ordered a mug of beer.

Not tipping his derby nor even saying hello, Marvin
Bohn drew the beer, looked at Red and accepted his
usual headshake, then set the mug in front of me.

"What's a man to do?" he asked.

"Either get rid of that brass bed, or get a real female
entertainer," I said.

"You're all the same. I wish you'd change the subject,"
he said, his pale white, flat face reflecting the dim light
like a pearl, his wide mouth drawn down, his wolfy dark
eyes set deep. "Why don't you talk about something

19

interesting like the grass growing or the price of dried beans?"

"How about dry-gulchin'?" I said, then wondered why the room went quiet.

Now I could see in the dim light that Bud Mabry was playing poker with Dutch Feldcamp, who had once been a pretty fair rider, but now would take about any kind of ranch work he could get; Wayne Farnhorst, the harness maker; Wade Filson, the blacksmith; and Ace Dietjen, the roader.

Down at either end of the long bar were other rannies who might not take kindly to talk about dry-gulching.

Among them was a hollow-cheeked older man who looked as if he hadn't ducked his head in a water bucket since last fall. The grayish stubble on his sunken features looked sore and raspy. His eyes were hidden under the scoop of his brow, and his long, greasy hair looked as if it had been trimmed with a cleaver.

He was leaning with ragged elbows on the bar staring at the drink in front of him, and without moving his body, he turned his shaggy head like a tumbleweed a quarter turn, looked up our way, and nodded.

"Howdy, Salty," I said, pretending I hadn't heard the news. "How's things over in Prayer Valley?"

He shook his head without answering and looked down at his glass again.

Salty Salkeld was our nearest neighbor to the southeast, but we didn't visit much. I wouldn't ever stop long enough there to eat because he was so dirty and butchered close to the house, so there was always a line of buzzards settin' on the fence and a stink worse'n a squaw on a gutwagon.

Marvin Bohn leaned over and mopped the bar in front of me and murmured without moving his lips, "Salty sold out to Tee-Bar last week."

"What's that got to do with dry-gulchin'?" I asked, just so nobody would figure I was backin' down.

"Murder's no joke," Marvin Bohn said clearly. "Folks have had a bellyful of it."

"I don't have a long rifle," I said easy as I could, "and I got nothing against mustangers, bein' one myself."

"Me, too," Red said with his back to the bar and his thumbs in his vest pockets.

"Folks are getting touchy," Frank Pedragal, the drayman, said. He'd been a stagecoach driver once, but he claimed the hard bouncing year after year shook his guts down and out, and he had to quit.

"I ain't callin' out any names, but we can be pretty damn certain it's Juniper," Bud Mabry said, studying his cards.

I glanced at Red and then looked back toward Mabry and Pedragal.

If you figured Pedragal looked like an old dominicker hen from the way his chest had slumped down to his belly and, with his front teeth gone, his chin was apt to graze his long nose, then you'd think of Bud Mabry as a Rhode Island Red rooster, tall and big boned, always on the peck with his reddish brown hair laying back over his head like feathers.

I never made up my mind as to whether Mabry was thickheaded or whether he talked with the purpose of keeping himself above everybody else. Either way I never much cottoned to him, not being inclined to give ground to a cowboy no better'n me.

"You're right, Frank," I said to Pedragal. "We don't get much news out home, but when somebody comes along and says something, we don't ask him to say it twice."

"What's your drift, Wes?" Dutch Feldcamp looked up from his cards.

"He said once we don't have no long rifle," Red said.

"Dally down, boys," Marvin Bohn said, getting a little color in his pearly cheeks. "Wes and Red live clear on the other side of the valley."

I was watching Mabry, hoping he'd look up at me and

make another remark so I could pile him, but he pretended the game was more interesting until I let out my breath and turned back to the bar.

"Need the Pinkertons," old Fly Swinner murmured from the end of the bar. He seemed to have staked out the place some years back and never left it whether he had money or not.

Sometimes he swept out the place in the mornings or did some service for Marvin Bohn, and for that he could steal a couple whiskeys that would keep him warm until he could mooch some more. Marvin Bohn never lost anything letting him camp out down at the end of the bar. A small old-timer, he wore a ratty goatee and a ragged gray mustache. His face had that pallid bloat of men you see who are drinking and doing nothing else. It generally means Grandfather Pneumonia will carry them off next winter.

"Hard to watch five hundred square miles of sagebrush," Ace Dietjen drawled. "It takes me a month to cover it."

"I don't know why folks won't say what everybody knows," Wade Filson muttered, slapping down his cards one at a time.

"How many so far?" I asked Marvin Bohn, now that they'd quit smellin' around my butt.

"All together . . ." Marvin said, drawing another beer, "all together over the years, I'd reckon about five."

The others nodded because everyone knew that number by heart.

"There's two one year, and two the next, then there wasn't any last year, like as if they'd learned maverickin' wasn't worth the candle," Frank Pedragal said in a singsong voice, as if he'd said the same thing a hundred times and still wasn't tired of it.

"Then Everett," Bud Mabry said, dealing the cards slowly because his big, callused hands couldn't feel the pasteboards.

"And they were all found over to the east," Dag Petersen put in with a spark of ferocity, which was all he had.

"Not exactly," Marvin Bohn said. "It'd be more like southeasterly or northeasterly."

No one would come out and say that all the killings had happened on the fringe of what Beecher Turnbull called his range. They were watching their words the way Aufdemburg weighed out his beans.

"Anyways, there ain't been any westerly, nor southwesterly or northwesterly," I said.

"It don't mean anything where they were," Wade Filson said. "Suppose somebody wanted to make trouble, maybe get an innocent man hung or bushwhacked?"

"He's takin' a helluva long time doin' it," Bud Mabry said, still keeping his eyes on his cards. "I reckon it's a lot more simple than that."

Marshal Witherspoon came in the door and automatically moved to the left so he wasn't silhouetted against the light, and when his eyes were adjusted to the gloom he came on to the bar and took a place by himself.

"Hot," he said, lifting his flat brown hat and wiping his bony forehead with his sleeve.

"In August you'll think this was cool," Marvin Bohn said, putting a beer in front of Witherspoon.

"This time of year the rattlesnakes go blind, shed their skins, and get twice as mean," Witherspoon said, glancing around. "I find it's the same with people."

"I don't see nobody around here strikin' out blind. Looks to me like everybody's settin' on their ass waitin' for the man with the long rifle to take over," Mabry said.

"You know I been over that ground plenty of times, and there ain't nothin' there to tie it on to anyone," Witherspoon drawled.

"Did you ask the man any questions?" Mabry came back at him, his anger strong enough to show.

"He said he didn't know anything about it."

"Maybe he'd sing a different song if somebody dry-gulched *his* kid brother," Mabry muttered.

"I hope you're not serious." Witherspoon turned so his right hand was hanging loose alongside the butt of his Remington .44.

Bud was going to have to put up or shut up if he kept on.

"I'm not a backshooter, Witherspoon," Bud said, never raising his eyes off the cards. "But I am some serious about justice for my kinfolk."

"I showed you the runnin' iron I found in Everett's boot. I doubt you'd defend a rustler."

"That iron was put in his boot afterward," Bud said flatly.

"I told you I walked a circle around his body, and the nearest tracks to him was five hundred yards away in the sandy coulee."

"That's what you told me all right," Bud said again, angrily slapping down his cards one at a time.

Marvin Bohn looked over at me and said loudly, "Wes, you hear about Rastus and Mandy goin' swimming?"

"No, reckon not."

"That Rastus was so dumb, when he saw Mandy come out of the swimming hole naked, he thought how pretty she'd look with clothes on."

He pretended to laugh, but except for turning the attention onto him, which I guess is what he wanted, the joke did nothing to lighten up the angry men.

Everyone knew why he did it, and after a minute of heavy quiet, they must have figured he was right.

"That reminds me of the one about the dummy who took his nose apart to see what made it run," Ace Dietjen smiled.

Old Dag Petersen down at the end of the bar laughed, and that finished the quarreling, for the moment anyways.

To me it was like no one wanted to say what was in

their heart, which was that Beecher Turnbull didn't waste time on a trial when it looked like there was some rustling about to happen.

It was as if they respected him in a way for handling the problem without disturbing anybody much, and yet it reminded them, too, that he could go ahead and do it without asking permission from anybody ahead of time.

The other thing was that the first four dead men were outsiders, drifters, strangers. Everett Mabry wasn't known for his good works exactly, but he was local, and it didn't set well for a local rider to be judged and executed without a trial.

It was too close. Maybe next time it would be one of us out looking for strays.

About then, when everyone was settling down to ordinary cattle and horse talk, the batwing doors popped open, and Beecher Turnbull himself crowded through, followed by a younger, smaller man.

Most everyone was smaller in one way or another than Beecher Turnbull. He'd been born big and he never slumped his broad shoulders to hide his extra height. Unlike a lot of big men who had problems with fat and pithy bones, Beecher had come up the hard way, bucking freight on riverboats when he was a kid, going on over to Texas where he probably did a considerable amount of mavericking, collecting enough unbranded cattle to make a drive to Virginia City, then drifting on west with the profit until he settled in Juniper Valley.

Most times he wore a frock coat and vest, but in deference to the heat he'd left off the coat and left his vest unbuttoned.

His black slouch hat looked brand-new, and the pearl-handled .36-caliber Colt hung as always on his right hip.

His eyes were set wide in his broad face. His big Roman nose was bent like a bow, and his thick lips rarely made a smile.

About the only bad thing you could say about his

appearance was that the years were catching up with him like everybody else. His short-cut hair was showing gray down around his ears, and the lines of his face were in so deep, the flesh was starting to droop over.

I thought that if he'd grow a beard, it would hide the jowls and wattles, but it was none of my business.

The young man behind him was dressed all in new working clothes—bulldogger boots, jeans, checkered shirt, and a tall, cream-colored Stetson. It was an outfit that would have gotten most dudes in trouble and made some fun for local punchers, but he was safe enough as long as he stayed close to his brother.

If Beecher Turnbull resembled his dad, the brother must have taken after their mother, for he was slender, with small bones and a thin face with wide cheekbones, each touched with a spot of red. His eyes were large, brown, and set wide like Beecher's. His hair was fine and yellow, and was neatly combed down in a scroll that came to within an inch of his collar, making him look like a dude, all right, but respectable enough as a man, and except for a wipe of grayness beneath his eyes, he seemed confident enough in himself.

They came in and settled in the empty space by me. Beecher didn't bother to introduce us.

"Hello," the young one said to me, "my name's Dan."

"Wes. And this is Red."

We shook hands while Beecher was ordering whiskey.

Already the kid brother was a helluva lot friendlier than Beecher had ever been, and I was about to ask him where he was from and bid him welcome to Juniper Valley, but Beecher had poured the glasses full of the forty rod that had been colored amber by soaking a plug of Climax chewing tobacco in the barrel.

"I'd rather have beer, Beech," Dan protested mildly.

"Beer is for drop calves," Beecher laughed, and lifted his glass. "Down the hatch."

He tossed down the whiskey, but Dan only touched it

to his lips for a taste, and said, "I'll go a little slower," setting the glass back on the bar.

The rest of the room was quiet except for the flutter of cards falling. Bud Mabry had quit trying to break the table by slapping them down one at a time, and it seemed everyone was either rolling a smoke, lighting a pipe, or cutting off a chew.

Normal times, me'n Red would figure it was time to pick up our provisions and ride on back out to the ranch, unless we had some serious celebratin' to do, which we hadn't had reason to yet today.

I looked at Red and tipped my head a fraction toward the street. It was a question that he answered by asking, "Care for another?"

"One more." I nodded and laid out a silver dime.

I wished we were down at the end of the bar with old Fly Swinner where we could watch the show, but it was too late to move. Later on I thought that if we'd been down there, Beecher Turnbull would have set up alongside of us anyways, so it didn't make any difference.

Marvin Bohn drew a beer for me, and young Dan said, "One for me too, please."

Beecher pretended he didn't notice it, but everyone else in that room saw that the kid was still trying to ride his own horse.

"Marvin," Beecher said loudly, "why don't you get some music in here? Hire an Irish tenor, or somebody can whistle bird calls."

"That's an idea," Marvin said, meaning nothing at all.

"Find a nigger can play the piano, or an injun with a tom-tom. Good Christ, it's like a tomb in here."

Looking at his bulky elegance, I could hardly believe he'd come off a river dock, worked the paddle steamers, and fought his way out of El Paso with his poke heavier than when he'd started, and then mastered mavericking in south Texas when dry-gulchin' became a part of that game.

"Peace and quiet bother you?" Bud Mabry drawled, studying his cards.

Turnbull was no fool. He registered the challenge without showing it, but he must have been thinking hell for leather. It wasn't in him to answer a question; he liked to set it up so it was him runnin' the show.

Meantime I was crowding Red down the bar an inch at a time, in case Bud Mabry was a real bad shot.

"Ever been in New Orleans?" Turnbull asked Bud.

"My name is Mabry, Bud Mabry," Bud said, glancing up for the first time.

"Your spread is just west of me," Beecher said as if expecting an answer. Bud said, "I'll take two," to Ace Dietjen, who was dealing.

"Anytime you want to sell, let me know," Beecher said clearly.

Bud pretended he didn't hear him, and tossed a chip in the pot.

He had old Turnbull by the tail and was screwing it down, but he didn't really know what to do after that. After a minute, Turnbull said sarcastically to Dan, "The man likes peace and quiet."

"Maybe it's the custom," Dan said.

"The best custom out here is the knockdown drag-out. I don't suppose they have that custom in Illinois anymore."

"No, Beech, thank heaven," Dan said, uncomfortable that he was being used like a puppet in a Punch and Judy show. "I'm ready to go back to the house."

I looked at Bud, smaller by a lot than Beech, but hard as a keg of horseshoes from punching cows and gathering mustangs, and I didn't think Turnbull would try any knockdown drag-out on him.

I felt a nudge from Red and followed his eyes, which were looking sideways at Bud Mabry's chair. There wasn't anything wrong with the chair, but it was easy to see that Mabry wasn't wearing his gun.

I quit crowding Red and settled down to finish my beer.

"There's men out here, Dan," Beecher said conversationally to his brother, "that were lucky to come in early and take up the water and the good land, but they never could do anything with it."

Turnbull waited for Dan to respond with the obvious question, but Dan closed up like an armadillo in a coyote den.

"You want to know why?" Turnbull kept on. "It's because they're too lazy to get off their butts and too ornery to let another man make something of it."

Mabry looked at his cards, but his wrinkled neck was getting red as rooster comb.

"Your play," Wade Filson said to him.

"Give me a minute, for Christ's sake," Mabry snapped back.

Turnbull turned to face the table again, hooking his elbows on the bar, watching Mabry closely.

"Name me a price, Mabry, and I'll take that devil's sandpile off your hands."

Mabry had had enough. His face was close to purple and his hands were trembling so much, he laid his cards down and said, "I fold." Then he looked up at Turnbull and said, "There's a lots of Mabrys from here clear on back to Tennessee, and when one of them falls, we all care about it."

"What's that supposed to mean?" Beecher spoke so quietly it was like he was trying to gentle an outlaw bronc.

"It means you shouldn't have killed Cousin Everett."

I don't think Bud Mabry really finished the sentence, because while Beecher Turnbull was looking as calm and relaxed as a pup in a basket, he was also bending his knees and turning a little to the right, and about when Bud Mabry thought he could say his piece, Beecher was springing off his toes, his knees were unwinding, and his right arm—powered by the massive shoulder—was un-corking.

The blow smacked Bud Mabry forward of his left ear, and sent him and his chair skidding all the way to the door.

Not a sound came from Mabry as he fell. Maybe he thought Turnbull would give him a little warning, ask him out to the alley or something more or less civilized, but he never had a thought after that for better'n an hour. Chances were the cheekbone was cracked because imme-diately a big knot sprouted up and turned blue. His eyes were closed and his breathing was a cross between a snore and a wheeze. A man could kill a young bull with that blow, if his fist would hold up to it.

There was that long space of silence where no one knows what's happened or what to do about it. There was the frozen picture of Beecher Turnbull poised in a crouch, both hands extended, his head pushed forward, a grin on his wide mouth and the whites of his eyes showing, then it broke apart. Turnbull dropped his hands, backed up to the bar, and seeing no fight in the bystanders, turned to Marvin Bohn.

"Whiskey for the house!"

Then turning to his brother, where I could see his face clear, he laughed, "They got Mabrys from here to Tennessee, but . . ."—he dragged out the words—". . . they . . . are . . . some . . . slow!"

Doc Meredith came in and undid Mabry's belt and listened to his chest, then looked at the blue dome forming on the side of his face.

Looking up at Turnbull, Doc said, "Looks like he's been hit by an eight-pound maul."

"It was a fair fight," Turnbull said. "He suggested I killed his cousin, but he couldn't back up his bullshit."

Dan, in the background, studied the floor.

Marshal Witherspoon came out of the dark corner holstering his six-gun. He looked hard at Turnbull and glanced around at the rest of us.

"It maybe wasn't so fair, but that's the way it was."

Neither me nor Red had any stake in it, which is to say we had no liking for either one of them. No one had anything to say when Turnbull and his fragile brother Dan stepped around the unconscious Mabry and went outside.

3

AT DAYBREAK, RED PACKED UP THE MULE HE HAD NAMED Beau. I couldn't get near the lineback brute. I'd traded Ace Dietjen a fair-looking gelding for him, partly because Ace said he was a good strong mule, and partly because my horse had a short memory so at least half the time, he'd go the wrong way.

The damned mule had been so sleepy and docile when I looked him over that later on I figured Ace must have chloroformed him some before he showed him to me.

Now he either wanted to take a bite off my arm if I come at him from the front, or whirl and kick at the same time if I tried him from the side. My shirt and vest were beginning to look like doll rags after a couple of times trying to put a pack on him, so I did the next best thing and turned him over to Red.

I suggested he win Beau's friendship with a clout on his solid head with a pick handle, but Red didn't even smile at my old joke. He left the mule tied to the gatepost all night without feed or water. The next morning he said something to the beast, untied him, and led the gentle Beau into the corral where he could drink and eat.

We keep the camp simple. A couple small tarps, frying pan, coffeepot, a cast-iron Dutch oven, a couple tin plates and cups, then our provisions in flour sacks that later serve as towels, too. Add a couple blanket-wrapped canteens and the bedrolls, some rolled-up rawhide latigo and plenty of extra ropes, and we were ready to travel over to the head of Prayer Valley.

They say that country got its name because a Mormon tried farmin' it and claimed he could grow corn if he prayed hard enough. He never said anything when he left.

We rode off to the southeast with me ahead because Red had to lead the mule. The country was drying up fast under the August sun, but we'd gathered and shipped out enough mustangs to leave some grass for the rest.

We cut off east before ever getting to the mouth of the little valley that opened into big Juniper, because we didn't want to disturb the homestead there, no matter who owned it now.

After the Mormon had discovered the spring and built his stone cabin, he went up the canyon and blasted out a hole so he could get the water to come out higher up for irrigation. Trouble was, his blast changed the underground flow so it dried up at his house and came out in several places about five hundred yards on down in the rocks.

Salty Salkeld had tried to make a go of it, but he'd starved out and sold his claim to Beecher Turnbull.

There was another seep that fed into a rock *tinaja* a mile or so back up the pinched-out valley that held enough water for the herd of mustangs that ranged there, and that's where we were headed.

The seep was well away from the old homestead and for sure on public land, but we still preferred to go in the back way over a low saddle in the rimrock, figuring it better to let sleeping dogs alone.

We'd trapped and taken fifteen head of unbranded mustangs out of there the year before and I was hoping we could bring out enough this time to pay for the upcoming winter in Mexico.

"They say on down there, there's jungle with monkeys and bananas and such," I said as we slowly climbed toward the saddle.

"I heard the people lay back in a hammock in the shade and eat pineapples and drink beer all day," I went on.

"Reckon we could do that?"

"It don't sound too hard."

"Or do they hate the gringos for chasin' out old Santa Anna?"

"I'm not worryin'," I said. "If you can sweet-talk that mule into submission, I reckon you can pacify plenty señoritas."

"I only need one."

"Don't forget your pardner," I said. "What are you, an Indian giver?"

"You worry too much, Nez." His eyes sparkled. "I'll get you a bride as good as Thelma Parker, maybe two."

"No, if that's the best you can do, I wouldn't feel right about sampling the local product. Maybe it'd be better to buy a bigger stove, stay home, and watch the icicles grow."

We reached the saddle, a barren slab of rotten granite, and stopped to look down into the winding, narrow valley, which was mostly dry, but had enough flats and box canyons for grass.

To the east, where it opened into Juniper country, I could see the boxy outline of the stone cabin, and a little smoke curling up.

Maybe we could be seen skylighted from the cabin, but I was disinclined to hide. Even if somebody'd moved into Salty Salkeld's place, we were as close to our ranch as we were to the Tee-Bar. So I kept telling myself, but deep down I felt a nervous shiver as I could imagine a jasper layin' off yonder with a buffalo rifle linin' up my shoulder blades.

I kneed my buckskin impatiently and led on down from the rimrock.

"Don't like the view?" Red asked, meaning something different.

"I'm leanin' toward Mexico," I said, feeling like a brush-skulking yeller dog.

It's not so bad fighting someone you can see or hear or smell or know he's there, but there ain't no fight with a dry-gulcher.

I didn't enjoy that fear corkscrewing my backbone either.

In normal times, I'd've split off by myself, ridden a long circle, and made a dry camp until I caught the sonofabitch and killed him, whoever he was.

But pride or greed got in the way. I wanted twenty sound horses from the reaches of Prayer Valley and meant to take them.

As I worked it through my head, I decided a bush-whacker would think twice about shooting one of us, because the one left over would surely dog him down and make his dying slow and mournful.

"We'll have to stay together," I said over my shoulder.

"It figures," Red agreed, "or you can ride around carryin' a white flag."

"Any day," I said, knowing he was teasing me but feeling the bitter truth of it, too.

We came into our old camp in a group of black oaks where it was cool during the day. Even though it was downwind of the *tinaja,* we wouldn't light a fire until we'd caught our horses, and we'd hold the noise down.

Chances were the mustangs already knew we'd arrived, but they wouldn't be overly spooked unless we made them that way.

After we watered and picketed the animals, we chewed

on some jerky and cold corn bread and finished it off with a couple cinnamon rolls Red had baked the day before. By then it was early dark.

At daybreak we took the mule and horses to the long rock tank where the wild ones had watered in the night, and then, with the coil of rawhide strapping and short axe, we commenced patching up the trap we'd used the year before.

It was set up in a draw upstream from the *tinaja* and didn't amount to much more than a corral enclosing the flat land, made of piñon poles tied to scrub oak or other piñons. It had a wide gate at the mouth, then a short runway that pinched down and opened into the main corral.

The idea was to put a rider below the *tinaja* and another rider above it off to one side, and when the wild horses came in the night to drink, the rider on the upper side would move down into the middle of the arroyo and block the herd long enough to spook them into the side draw.

Once through the wide gate, they'd go on through the runway gullet into the corral, where they'd mill around while we secured the first gate. Later on we could close the smaller gate at the entrance of the corral.

It would work if the mustangs weren't already too spooked to come down and drink. Some of those hammerheads could hold off three or four days without water if they thought there was something contrary going on, and then they'd hightail it someplace else.

I cut and trimmed piñon poles while Red worked around putting them in where the old ones had rotted away, and replaced some of the rawhide ties. Pretty much most of the trap was still in good shape, and we finished before dark.

It was another cold camp with simple fare, a part of the mustangers' regular living. That wasn't so bad if you figured in the smell of piñon and junipers floating down the canyon, the cooing of small doves at nightfall, and the dark range of mountains silhouetted against the dying sun that still fired the western tailings of somber, vagrant clouds overhead.

I always figure an Indian has the edge on me in his extra perceptions, so I asked Red if he'd noticed anything.

"Maybe he don't know we're up here," Red said, and shook his head.

"I don't cotton to the notion we're hiding and working undercover."

"Can't do nothin' about it now," Red said, closing the subject.

Just before dark, Red rode his Appy on a roundybouty way to his station well above the *tinaja* and I took the buckskin up to where the rocks pinched in below into a narrow trail, and by waiting on a boulder there, blocked off the lower valley. Of course the horse herd could escape by running crosswise up the steep slopes and around, but it was their nature to want to go back up to their regular grazing in the broken *barrancas* and *malpaís*.

Buck, saddled and ready, waited there in the last of the twilight with me, patient as a tree, while my thoughts roamed on to small things in the past.

Things like being a barefoot kid riding calves on my folks' farm in Missouri, along with my brother. Going to church and meeting up with other farm boys, nobody saying anything, everyone being so shy, but there was a good feeling about those days with Ma and Pa holding us all together, him using some salty language and a willow switch, and her using wild plum pies and molasses spice cakes. It seemed then that we were all together on the right path and nothing would ever happen to turn it around.

But then came the war, and though we didn't have any slaves, and didn't know anyone who did, we were still in the wrong place what with General Price chasing General McCullough, and Grant chasing Pillow . . . somehow

I recalled the story about General Pillow building a fortified line down in southern Missouri and putting the ditch on the wrong side . . . and General Sam Curtis chasing General Prentiss clear to Arkansas, and right smack dab in the middle of it was the Bengard farm that just disappeared as food for the troops and fuel for their campfires, ending up with Pa shot dead, Ma dead from fever, brother Bill joined up and lost at Shiloh or Pittsburgh Landing, it was all the same human slaughtering ground, and me living off the scraps of either army until it was over.

Because I felt more comfortable with Southerners, I'd gone downriver instead of up, and found work on the big Hashknife Ranch, living life a day at a time after that, because there was no more Ma or Pa or solid home. I never had taken up with a woman, because I never had nothing but a Mexican saddle and a rusty six-gun.

Tried the sporters along the drive to the Musselshell in Montana, but there wasn't enough money in the world to keep one permanent. After enough foul talk, low-slung tits and droopy butts, I figured I was just spendin' my pay to hose out a big old well-used nauch so I slowed that sport down to a walk, and saved a few dollars.

Not much to remember from those days, except times when a rider's horse fell and broke a leg bad, or a killer bronc went over backwards and drove the saddle horn into Dusty Sheets, then got up and bucked him off. They burned the unlucky saddle on top of Dusty's grave.

Nothing much. Still I came through. Killed an Indian horse thief in Kansas, but never killed anybody in a street fight because I didn't take to drink all that much, and so never was that crazy.

No, there was that little runt of a self-appointed lawman thought he could push any knotheaded cowboy around. Missed his heart by three feet. After they cut his leg off, everybody called him Shorty and that was worse for him than being shot.

I thought some of the whiskey-haired girl that had been the schoolmarm at Buttonwillow until Beecher Turnbull had married her, and wondered if maybe someday I might find one like her. Likely not. Thelma Parker on my birthday was about the best I'd ever do.

Funny how that perky light brown ponytail stuck in my mind, and the way her blue eyes looked square into mine, sort of saying, "we're all in this crazy world together, Wesley," even though we hardly knew each other.

"I sure appreciate knowin' you, Wesley."

I heard wild horses up the defile from me. The mares holding back and milling, the stud coming forward, whistling, then dodging back for cover, rattling the rocks.

They knew we were around somewhere but they wanted to drink. I guessed they wouldn't settle down and come to drink at the stone tank until right before daybreak.

I sat there and wondered about living far down in Mexico. Not the border towns, where the cheap tequila drives men loco and the whores are cheap until you look in your wallet the next morning, but the country and the country people on south where life had to be true as a lookin' glass, and you earned your own respect.

Thinking about it, I figured there was no more future for a rider like me there than here in Juniper country, but at least it'd be interesting to see.

I dream of Jeanie with the light brown hair . . .

Rocks rattled on up above, the horses snorted and kicked at each other, disturbed but not fashed in a panic, and there was nothing for me to do but wait to head 'em off.

I could tell they were moving closer and I stepped quietly over to Buck, looped the reins over his head, and very slowly, to keep the leathers from creaking, climbed aboard. He waited patiently for a knee pressure, or a fist rolling on his withers, but I gave him nothing.

A faint shadowless glow lifted from the east and I

waited for the rush. They were drinking, bobbing their muzzles into the *tinaja,* no doubt completely alert and wary, ears pointing, heads moving, unshod hooves slipping on the slick rock, and I gauged we'd have daylight in a couple minutes.

If they would stay that long, Red could turn them. He couldn't do it in the dark because they'd roar on by him, but if they could see him and his slicker waving around, they'd likely turn.

They'd held off drinking so long it took them extra time, and there was plenty of light when I kneed Buck up over the path that twisted through the boulders.

There was no way a horse could get over me or over the rocks.

They heard me coming, because all of a sudden it was quiet as a treeful of owls up there, then I heard them milling about, then they scatted in one quick instant back up the way they'd come.

I heard their hooves clattering and I pushed Buck as fast as he could go in the narrow turnings, and I heard, far up the canyon, Red whistle and give a mild "yah! yah!" at the horses as they charged him.

If he could hold the passage . . . well, that's what he was supposed to do. If he couldn't, nobody else could, and so you would need to refigure the trap.

Clearing the boulders, I reached the rocked-up *tinaja* that was wet all about and the ground torn up, and put Buck into a hard trot now that there was room, and coming to where Red had turned them, kneed Buck to the left and found Red on foot dragging the pole and rawhide gate closed.

I helped him tie it shut. Leaving our horses, we walked slow down the gullet that pinched into the main corral, and scared back a couple smart mustangs who had the right idea but were a little late.

The inner gate was easy to shut and we looked through the poles at our new horse herd.

"How many you figure?" I whispered.

"Thirty, give or take a couple."

"Good work."

"There's a cripple and some mares with sucking colts."

"The big stud?"

"He's got a Tee-Bar brand on his shoulder."

"I don't see any other brands." I kept my voice down, wondering if the Tee-Bar would make us extra trouble. Turnbull could argue that all colts sired by his stud belonged to him—a smart trick if you could make it work.

"I missed a pair of mares last year," Red said quietly.

"Those with the foals yonder?"

"They're wearin' our brand," he nodded.

"Well, thanks, Mr. Turnbull, for the service."

Red didn't waste any time building a little fire and boiling the coffee. He likes to eat regular and, in general, better than most peelers, and we'd been on cold rations for a couple of days. I had a kind of dull, bottom-of-the-barrel feeling because of the long sleepless night, fretting about the past and the future like a mill wheel turning round and round but going nowhere.

Red boiled up a big pot of oatmeal mush with raisins and brown sugar and cinnamon stick in it, and that set pretty good. I began to feel human again and ready to go to work.

Opening the inner gate, going slow and easy, we cut the branded stud and the crippled colt out of the milling horses and ran them into the gullet, where I let them out the big Texas gate to freedom. The cripple had somehow twisted the hock on his front leg and it hadn't healed right, making him useless as a riding horse.

With his reata at his side, Red walked through the whirling brand of bright-colored horses and made a short overhand cast over the neck of one of our branded mares.

If she was branded, she'd been taught how to face a rope, and in a minute she remembered and stood still as

Red slipped a hackamore over her head, then made a half hitch on the bolsa with his lass-rope and patted her neck a while until she quit shaking and saw that the foal was close by. After pulling back and forth on the lead rope, he got her moving, and then it was easy to lead her down to the far end of the gullet and change the reata for a length of soft cotton rope and tie her to the rail so she could settle down some more.

The main idea was to cull out all but the wild ones so there'd be more room and less of a ruckus in the main pen. Red was better with horses than me, so I handled the gates, and made sure he had the right ropes and hackamores and headstalls, whatever he needed.

It was a pleasure to watch how quiet and careless he moved among the wild animals, any one of which could have killed him in an instant if they'd ever got the idea he was an enemy.

"With the *potros,* the slower you go, the faster you get there," he said over his shoulder as he went back into the swirling mass of mustangs.

When the next of our branded mares fought the rope he asked me to walk behind her as he kept the lead rope taut, and she went right along then with her eyes trying to roll back to see what I was doing.

He secured her to the rail next to the other mare, who was by now tired of pulling against the rope and had settled down to the sleepy lassitude of horse boredom.

Both foals were colts, and later on at the ranch we'd look them over and if there was nothing really exceptional about them, we'd cut and brand them and turn them out again to grow for a couple, three years more before bringing them back in. That is, if we were still alive in three years, or still in the Juniper Valley country. I wasn't planning that far ahead. Except that in running the horse business, you had to go by that kind of a system because horses don't grow any faster than that.

I suppose we could sell them as colts, but they

wouldn't bring enough to pay for the trouble, whereas three years from now, they'd be full grown and ready to go to work.

There was a hammerheaded chestnut stray amongst the bunch that bore a Circle C brand that was strange to our country. I decided to take him on in and ask around. If I couldn't find the owner I'd sell him to Ace Dietjen and let him worry about it.

Most any branded horse, no matter how long he's been out on the range, remembers he was caught by the rope once and he may not like it, but he'll settle down quicker than a plain wild mustang.

Of course, if the man who roped and branded him also clubbed him or hurt him for no reason, he'd remember that, too.

It's the chance you have to take. Red came up close, roped the Circle C gelding easy as pie and set back for the expected pull, but the gelding just flattened his ears, bared his teeth, and charged at Red, crazier'n hell.

Red wasn't ready, and the horse struck him with a forefoot, knocked him down, and stepped on him as he went by.

Red let loose of the rope and curled up into a ball while I hurried out and made sure none of the milling horses kicked him just because he was something strange laying there.

"Sonofabitch is an outlaw," Red said, getting to his feet, his right arm hanging down. "He's got a tricky hook with that off forefoot." Red felt his shoulder with his left hand. "That's why he's strayed this far—nobody wants him."

"Can you feel your right hand?" I asked.

"No, but it'll come back in a while."

He gimped over to the gate and stood guard, kneading his shoulder all the time, while I walked through the horses and caught the reata dragging after the outlaw, slipped through the corral poles, and took a couple turns high up around a black oak that was serving as a fence post.

He squealed and grunted and fought the rope, but about the time he was ready to choke down, he'd come close to gain some air and I took up the slack. After a while I had him snubbed up close to the fence.

Tying off the reata, I let him stay where he was. He could fight the rope all he wanted, wear off some hide and get a stiff neck out of it, but sooner or later, he'd have to calm down.

I took over the roping while Red tried to get his arm working again. There wasn't any wrangler better than Red, so I didn't pretend to be any better than I am, which is about fair to good.

I caught a big gray stud, maybe a two-year-old, probably the son of the Tee-Bar stallion, and worked him through the system the same as Red had done with the mares. I couldn't get him settled down enough for the hackamore, so I took a turn around a post and choked him until his eyes were starting to roll up, then I pushed him over, slacked the noose, slipped on the hackamore before he was fully conscious, stepped back, and let him get up. He fought the rope a while until his neck and nose got sore, then he took a step forward and decided to think it over. I left him tied where he was, and with another reata, went out and caught another one on the other side of the corral. This one was another son of the Tee-Bar stud, a strong horse who wore me out pulling this way and that, until I got him snubbed and choked down.

Sweat was running down into my eyes and I rambled over to Red where he was guarding the gate, hunkered down on my heels, and took off my hat.

"Some hot."

"They're comin' around."

"Sure. How's your arm?"

"It'll get better or I'll cut it off."

"What about that outlaw?"

"Leave him tied to the oak until we're done."

"Then what?"

"After we leave, you can come back and shoot him."

"My feelings exactly," I said. "There's too many good horses in here to waste a year fightin' that one."

"'Course, you could turn him loose."

"And maybe he'd stray over to the Tee-Bar and kill the boss." I smiled.

"Likely it'd be some poor raggedy-ass peeler," Red said.

Rested up some, I fetched out another reata, caught and tied a calico filly, then led the gray stud from the corral into the gullet, with Red walking behind him, and tied him with a soft rope next to the mares.

By rotating them that way, letting a fresh one fight the rope until he learned he was hurting himself, while catching up another one and leading the tamest one into the gullet, we managed to have a dozen horses tied side by side.

"Dinnertime," Red said as I tied a strong four-year-old mare in the gullet and stopped for a breather.

"Fine with me."

"You don't think someone will see the smoke?" Red asked carefully.

"I don't give a damn."

Red busied himself with his pots and pans and before long he had a big pot of macaroni with chunks of ham and some tasty spices in it. Between us we ate it all. I thought I was full until he poured a cup of coffee and brought out a bag of gingersnaps.

We drowsed a spell in the shade until Red felt lightened up enough to get on his feet. I'd as soon spent the afternoon snoozing comfortable that way.

I thought about Beecher Turnbull and his wife with the whiskey-colored ponytail having dinner in the big house. Likely Mrs. Snapp would put the china plates and bowls and platters on a shiny white tablecloth. Then I remembered the brother, Dan. Where would he be sitting? Between Beecher and Jean Louise. I had the sudden notion that they'd better get another female sitting at that table before Jean Louise thought to compare the two brothers.

It was an idle glimmer in my drowsy mind, but it made me think that Beecher Turnbull might be a little extra bronco on account of some such scene.

Red's arm was working again even though there was a big knot on his shoulder that would hurt him for a week. He took on the roping while I talked and gentled down the ones that had learned to face the rope quietly. Some learned quicker than others, but between Red's calm, quiet way of doing the job, and my doing the drudge part, we managed to have twenty-eight good horses broke to the rope by nightfall.

"I wish we could water 'em," he said as darkness crowded over the canyon, "but it'd take all night to teach 'em to drink out of a bucket."

"They'll be all the more willing to travel in the morning," I said, wondering how far the glow of our campfire could be seen. I'd been expecting a visit from Turnbull or a line rider all day, and the fact that no one came made me edgy.

The fragrance of the piñons drifted down into the box canyon, and we listened to the owls and coyotes for a while, but my old carcass was aching from handling the horses, and I nodded off with my saddle under my head.

Sometime in the middle of the night I heard nickering and the stamping of hooves, slipped on my boots, and trotted over toward the corral with my six-gun in hand.

"Easy, Wes," Red said out of the darkness.

He was standing by the outer gate; his high-crowned hat that had once been white shone more than his face.

"What is it?" I asked quietly.

"That Tee-Bar stud wants his harem back."

46

I heard his hoofs clattering as he charged through the rocks and brush farther up the canyon. Then he split the soft air with a demanding whistle and grunting. Pacing back and forth, he kept up the short bursts of whinnying and snorting, and was answered by the melancholy whickering of his harem individually tied inside the corral.

If we weren't there he'd come on in and kick the gate down and get them out one way or another, but he was shy of us, which all added up to no more sleep for the rest of the night.

"Build up the fire," Red said. "That'll bother him and I can make some coffee."

I brought our own picketed horses in closer to camp in case the stallion went after them, too, built up the fire, then went back and relieved Red at the gate.

The stud was still sending signals to his band, but other than making them nervous, did nothing much more than wear himself out.

I didn't think we'd caught his entire band because there's always some that hold back or they're off looking someplace else. He'd pick up another harem soon enough. Maybe in a couple years we'd come back to this little canyon in the great Juniper range and pick up his get again.

Red brought me a cup of coffee and we stayed with the horses until the first light of dawn.

As soon as he could see well, Red went down and brought back Beau, the mule, hitched our bedrolls over the paniers, and by sunup we had secured the wild ones together in two groups, each bunch tied to a lead line.

One of the bands was tied to the mule, the other was dallied to my saddle horn. Red on his Appaloosa stayed behind to keep them from balking.

The stud had given up and gone with daylight.

I led the way on an angle up the slopes to the rocky saddle, the way we had come in, and dropped on down to the flats. It wasn't easy at first. Despite their stiff, sore necks, they wanted to balk or stampede, but because of the way they were tied they spent most of their strength fighting against each other. They could never get organized enough for all of them to pull against the single lead line at one time. If they had, they'd have dragged me clear to Buttonwillow, but without the Tee-Bar stallion telling them what to do it was in their nature for each one to act on his own.

We cleared the timber and walked slowly across the grassland, aiming for home, when I felt a tug on my shirt collar and my neck burn, then heard the scream of a bullet, followed by the distant boom of a rifle echoing off from the side of the mountain.

Red came at a gallop, and I quickly passed over the lead lines and whirled the buckskin half around.

"Don't be crazy, Wes!" Red snapped out before I leaned over Buck's neck and gave him the go-ahead.

Buck leaped like a jackrabbit so quick and strong it probably saved his life, because another rifle ball came screaming in right where he'd been a second before. Then he gobbled up the flat land with his huge strides while I felt for the stock of my saddle gun, making sure it was in its scabbard, and unlimbered my Colt .44.

The second shot gave me a line and I put Buck on a straight course for the covert up on a sidehill in the oaks.

Even though I was probably out of range, I commenced firing where I thought the bushwhacker was holed up, hoping to unsettle him if he was planning another shot.

There's only one way to fight a sniper and that's to drive on him so fast he'll run. You know already he's yellow and you can figure he'll lose his nerve and make mistakes when he sees you riding at him full blast.

'Course, if you're wrong, and he's halfway level, he'll

put a bullet through your horse's chest and watch you land on your head.

It don't matter. The main thing is you can't live your normal life if there's some skunk going to shoot you in the back when he takes a notion.

Got to do something about it. Best finish it quick.

At the edge of the oak grove an old log lay moldering away, and I jumped Buck over it, ready to fire.

Nothing moved.

I let Buck stand, his breath coming hard and rasping, climbed down from the saddle with the .44 in my hand, and studied the ground.

There were the marks of his boots where a man had kneeled behind the log. I sighted over and saw Red in the distance, about a thousand yards by now, leading the strings of mustangs at a walk across the valley floor. I checked the oak duff and saw the brass glint in the sun. The cartridge case was a long bottleneck and was stamped on the end with ".38-55." That and a faint smell of burned powder was all.

I found where his sidekick had held his horse, but I lost their trail in the rock slabs that made a notch in the rimrock.

Nothing for it but to get back to Red before he turned loose the horses and came looking for me. I wasn't sure he would do that, but I didn't want to take the chance of losing our Mexican vacation on a wild-goose chase.

Easing off Buck's canter, I brought him down to an easy trot so he could get his breath and not scare the broncs.

Red looked at me without saying anything.

"One man with a .38-55, another holding the horses."

"That's all?"

"Lost 'em on the rock."

"Son of a bitch—"

"Nothin' lost," I said.

"These broncs are learning fast, and soon as they smell the water at the ranch we'll pick up the pace." Red nodded, passing the lines back to me.

"Who you reckon it was?" I asked, kind of put out that he didn't seem too worried about my ruined shirt collar.

"I don't believe it was some old prospector who's discovered a ledge of gold a foot wide."

"Why don't you just say it out?" I growled.

"Because it don't seem fit. 'Course he started out poor and scrabbled his way to be boss bull of the valley, and likely laid down a few jaspers doin' that, but it's still open range and his headquarters is fifteen miles the other way."

"So there's somebody he's payin'."

"It ain't somebody paid by the head, because it don't happen regular, more like it was . . ."

". . . an impulse," I put in. "A couple line riders see somebody, know what the boss wants and deliver it from so far away there's no chance of bein' caught."

"Still, it don't add up, does it? Big man. Got the money. Got the big house, the pretty little wife. Seems like he's already got everything," Red said.

"He don't have any kids," I murmured, thinking of that cheery fair-skinned girl with the light brown ponytail. Her eyes were the same blue as her shawl.

The wooden water trough in the corral next to the windmill was full, but it still took some time to get those wild horses to enter the corral. Finally, while I held the strings, Red led them in one at a time until there were more drinking and splashing in than out, and then all those outside wanted to be inside.

Once they were in and the gate closed, the sun was laying out like a broken egg yolk on the horizon, and I headed for the cabin.

" 'Quittin' already?" Red asked.

"Let me know when breakfast is served," I said, and went inside, shucked off my boots, took off my hat, and crawled into my bunk.

I didn't hear Red come in and fire up the stove. I was plain tired out, so much so I didn't even worry about it or my old age.

4

I WOKE UP SMELLING SOMETHING HEAVENLY BAKING IN THE oven of the old nickel-plated range, and despite the stiffness in my old joints and the incidental bruises that come from knocking around with wild horses, I put on my hat and my boots, went outside without saying anything, and washed my whiskery face until I considered myself ready to face the day. I felt the left side of my neck but the burn was gone.

I changed my shirt to be sure I was remembering right and saw the hole through the left side of the collar. At six hundred yards, he'd missed the bull's-eye by about eight inches, which to my mind was pretty fair shooting.

Back in the kitchen, I sat on an old wired-together chair and watched Red peeking into the oven.

"What are you makin'?"

"Apple strudel," he said over his shoulder. "I'll fry up some eggs and sowbelly soon as it's done."

I poured myself a cup of coffee and took my seat again. "I'm goin' to be too contented to go to Mexico."

"Wait'll them chilly winds blow and you got to take an axe out every mornin' to chop water."

"I guess I been broke to pastry," I said. "If you mean to go, I don't have any choice."

"It ain't so hard you can't learn yourself." Red used a flour sack wrapped around his hand to lift out the baking pan with a nicely browned strudel in it.

Putting the pan up in the warming oven, he set an iron skillet over the front stove lid, poked a piece of wood into the firebox, and started slicing bacon.

"You know what's the three important parts of a stove?" he asked, concentrating on the bacon.

"No, I don't," I said, although he told the damn joke about once a month.

"Lifter, leg, and poker," he said without cracking a smile on that little hard face inside the big round face.

"That's all right," I chuckled, because I could already see this day was going to be better'n the day before.

"I didn't make it up myself."

"Well, it's a new one on me."

After breakfast, I helped wash up while the day was still climbing on sunrise. We went down to the first holding corral, where the wild ones, still wearing their headstalls and cotton ropes, were milling around uncertainly. Their lead ropes dragged in the dirt so that whenever one horse's lead rope was stepped on by another he'd get his head jerked, and they were learning all by themselves to keep their feet away from the ropes. The rest of their lives they'd know better than to get tangled up in their picket ropes and cut their legs.

By now their heads were sensitive and their necks sore enough so they didn't want to argue with the rope.

Any one of them now would stop and face the wrangler if he put a loop over his head. That was about half the training they needed to start off.

Looking over the young stallions still in the pen, I asked, "You see any studs in there worth keeping entire?"

"There's the blue roan that looks a lot like his daddy."

"He's got a nose like a wolf."

"What do you think?"

"Better to cut him now than later."

Red built a fire, fed it until he figured there were enough coals, then put a couple Lazy B irons in the fire, while I worked one of the young studs over his way.

Red came out with his reata, forefooted the colt, caught the hind foot and tied it close up to the front feet, then ran the rope up under his shoulder so the colt had only one hind leg free.

"Now," he said, and shoved his burly shoulder against the colt's and pushed him over. I went with him, holding his head up so he couldn't get his feet under him, and in a couple seconds Red had his other hind leg feet tied and the colt was laying there pretty much helpless.

Red moseyed over to the fire, brought back a cherry red iron, touched it carefully to the colt's shoulder, marking him for life as having been one of our own. After putting the iron back in the coals, he got out his jackknife, opened the castrating blade, kneeled by the hind end, and taking his time despite the rage and fear of the colt, made a cut, pulled out the balls so the cord was stretched tight, then a touch with the blade and the horse was a gelding.

Tossing the bloody testicles into a bucket, he asked conversationally, "Care for Juniper Mountain strawberries for supper?"

"Not me," I said, holding the colt's head up. "I'll settle for apple strudel."

He undid the half hitches, and when the rope was clear of the gelding's feet, I let the pressure off his head and scooted clear.

Red didn't hold much with pine tar, ashes and water, purple oil, lard, or any other disinfectants for the wound.

"Nature does it better the less we fool with it," he said.

It took us all morning to cut and brand the nine studs

and Red never got hurried up or discomforted whenever some little thing would go wrong, like a rope slipping, or heads knocking together, or switching tails. Slow and easy. Patience, patience, the slower you go the faster you finish. He didn't work at trying to be something he wasn't. He went at that same pace all day, no matter what.

About noon, when we were washing off the horse dung and blood, fixing to take time off in the heat of the day for dinner, Babe Silliman came into the yard driving his spring wagon that was fitted out to show his sewing machine samples as well as to provide a place to eat and sleep.

Babe was a tall, well-built Kentucky boy with a soft, mellow voice, curly black hair and big brown spaniel eyes that could get him through any lady's front door. Yet beneath that gray frock coat and behind those shiny, wet eyes was a man who'd plowed a lot of poor ground before he run up too many matrimonial debts and discovered that skedaddling, no matter how much it shamed him, was more prudent than bigamy.

In his wanderings he must have seen a lot and heard a lot that most folks generally miss, because although there were those fine little laugh lines around his eyes and dimples in his cheeks, there was still something inside him like a dark curtain that sometimes closed and you wouldn't know if his silence came from heartbreak or an awful cynical despair.

After we'd made our greetings and asked him in to eat, we kidded him some about not needing a sewing machine because all we ever used for mending was rawhide and we doubted whether his machine could handle such a material.

"I wouldn't be too sure," he smiled. "These new Grover and Baker machines can do anything except shoe horses, and they're workin' on that."

Red mixed up a Virginia molasses pie in a hurry and

put it in the oven, then fried some thin sliced beef in tallow, boiled potatoes, and made brown gravy from the steak drippings.

"You boys always eat like this?" Babe drawled, wiping his plate clean with half a flaky biscuit.

"Except when I cook," I nodded.

"When do you cook?"

"Haven't started yet," I said, "because I never cuss at mealtime."

The molasses pie was extra tasty from the nutmeg Red had grated onto it.

"No wonder you rannies never come to town." Babe belched politely. "Mind if I stay on for a year or two? I can darn and sew pretty fair."

"Sure. Just remember the cook keeps his scalpin' knife handy, like if you forget to smile one day, you're goin' to lose your hair."

"Him," Red said, jabbing his butcher knife in my direction, "he don't know the difference between rhubarb pie and cow pie."

"What *is* the difference?" I asked, and he threw the knife. It stuck in the wall about a foot over my head.

"You see what I mean?" I grinned.

"I oughta quit," Red said.

"I'm sure you could hire on at the big house," Babe said innocently.

"I don't suppose Jean Louise learned much about cookin' from teachin' school," I said to lead him on.

"No, and of course she comes from those poor Raffertys that never had much more than a cold potato for dinner anyway," Babe said. "Worked her own way through school washing clothes, and that sure didn't leave much time for the culinary art."

"Maybe that kid brother can show her something," I suggested.

"Possible . . ." Babe glanced my way with his big brown eyes looking innocent as a dove. "Beech wants to make him into a cowboy."

"Looked to be a lunger," Red said from the corner where he was scouring his pots and pans.

"Might be," Babe said. "It's true enough he's sick in bed more than most."

"Nice-lookin' fellow," I said. "Nicely set up, probably smart, too."

"What do you suppose did he study to be?"

"Likely the law," I said. "Turnbull is goin' to need a lawyer in the family."

"How do you figure?" Babe asked idly, tipping back in his chair and putting his shiny boots on the wood box.

"He's claimin' open range as his own. It ain't legal."

"I doubt if he's paying taxes on it," Babe allowed.

"Then there's some say he pushes on his next-door neighbors so hard with his hired guns on the prod all the time, he don't have too much trouble buying them out."

"He does carry a few extra hands on the payroll that don't seem to do much except ride around checking brands and calling on folks."

"Then there's dry-gulching—"

My word seemed to hang in the air as Babe got out his jackknife and commenced paring his fingernails.

"It's customary to kill rustlers," he said after a while.

"But it's not legal," I said. "If it ain't legal, it's murder."

"That's pretty strong." Babe sighed like he was carryin' a heavy burden.

"I've got a new shirt with a bullet hole through the collar," I said. "I wonder what Jean Louise would charge to wash and mend it."

"I don't guess I'd get that close to the fire," Babe said, as Red looked over his shoulder at me, anger in his eyes.

"Still and all, the shirt is ruined and I'm some disappointed."

"I travel all around the Juniper country, you know, and I hear things the way you can hear a stampede, by putting your ear to the ground."

"What do you hear?"

"It seems a lot of the folks feel about the same as you, not so much from riders being ambushed, as the way he crowds folks out instead of lending a hand."

"Comes over, makes a little pissy-assed offer, they say no, then Dee comes over and scares the women. Then there's an argument and they sell out after that. Seems it's worked out step by step," I said plain out.

"If it was me, I wouldn't start a one-man war I couldn't win," Babe said.

"But it comes back down to my ruined shirt. I only got one more shirt, and if somebody puts a messy hole in the back, it's hard times."

"She's a lonely lady," Babe said sleepily, "and while I'm no judge of females, she strikes me as being dangerous."

"You're sayin' maybe brother Dan will make her feel a little less lonely?"

"What it indicates to me just now is that it's better to keep your shirt on and let the cards keep falling," Babe said, putting his boots down on the plank floor and rising easily out of the chair to his full height. "Much obliged, Red, for the dinner, and I appreciate the conversation, but I've got to deliver a sewing machine to a widow woman over in Lander County no later than tomorrow."

"Glad you came out of your way," I said.

"I had a hankerin' for Red's cooking," Babe said, the curtain drawn behind those shiny spaniel eyes.

As he drove his team of matched grays out of the yard and headed on west, Red said, "That's the best liar I ever heard."

"Yes, indeed," I muttered, thinking of that fresh-faced girl sitting between the two brothers.

We went on over to the big corral, where the wild bunch waited. The newly cut geldings were wilted down like they'd eaten second-growth Johnson grass and sick to die, but in a week or so they'd have their heads back up and the misery they felt just now would likely be forgotten.

Red looked at our pair of branded mares with their foals, keeping outside the bunched-up band. "Let's work them out and see what they've got first."

I was agreeable because I thought they'd be easier than the others who had never known a rope before yesterday.

I stayed close to the gate of the breaking corral while Red worked through the horses and eased one of the mares, a stockinged sorrel, toward the gate, and I stepped back so she'd pass on in without making a big ruckus about it.

The foal was a filly and tried to hide behind her big mother, but we pretended she wasn't even there.

Red dabbed a loop over the mare's head and she came quietly to the snubbing post. I brought over a leather blinder that could be pulled up or down on the hackamore, and Red eased alongside her, rubbing the leather on her shoulder and gradually working it to her head where she could see it and smell it. After he slipped it on the hackamore without bending her ears or bothering her in any way, he took the cotton rope around her neck that ran through the hackamore and tied it to the post.

Then he lifted a gunnysack off the fence and rubbed her neck with it, let her smell it, and tossed it under her neck and around her feet until she knew there was nothing to fear from it. I joined him with another sack and we played our sacks all over her body and around her head until she quit flinching and trembling.

We lowered the blind over her eyes, rolled up the sacks, and made hobbles for her front feet, and I pulled the rope around her near her hind foot so she couldn't kick when Red put the hobble on it and the other one.

I lifted up the blind and turned her loose from the snubbing post. Still hobbled, she tried to run away, but I jerked her off her feet and she fell with a thump to the sandy ground. In a short time she learned to respect the hobbles.

We sacked her down again, and taking off the hobbles, I showed her the saddle blanket and gently eased it over her back; then, with both of us chatting with her, Red slipped his swellfork single-rig saddle on top of the blanket. He hooked the hanging cinch ring on the off side with his boot toe and brought it under her to his hand, then gently tightened the cinch. Although her ears were back, she didn't try to break away.

"She's good," Red said.

"You mean to ride her?"

"Some," Red said, nodding.

The corral was big enough so that she felt free to run, but when Red took the hackamore reins and a couple fingers of her mane in his left hand, and stepped up in the stirrup to swing aboard, she didn't flinch or jerk away.

I mounted Buck and moved toward her, which gave her the idea to move, but the bucking had been pushed out of her head when we'd broken her to the hobbles, and Red rode her around the corral trying the rein on her some, but mainly getting her accustomed to carrying a rider without complaint. In a little while she was trotting around the corral with her head up and a loose rein.

"That'll do it for today," Red said, then reined her up and dismounted. Rubbing her neck, he talked to her a while, led her back into the other corral, stripped off the rig and hackamore, and turned her loose with her foal.

"That's one," Red said.

5

OFF AND ON THROUGH THE DAY, I THOUGHT ABOUT WHAT Babe Silliman had said and not said, and around sunset, after we'd finished sacking the second mare and giving her a short ride, I cleaned my old .44, oiled its innards, and wiped it down again so there was nothing slippery about the butt or the trigger.

"Mad now?" Red asked, putting some flour and sugar in his sourdough starter so it'd be ready by morning.

"I'm slow."

"Better that way. Need me?"

"I'd rather someone was here in case that big sonofabitch sends Gibbon to burn us out."

"He won't. Not yet," Red said.

"Knowin' you're here, he'll think twice."

"Best get it out of your craw, whatever it is," Red said, nodding.

I wondered what he meant after I crawled into my bunk. He knew as well as me that I was going to call on Beecher Turnbull and get our business straightened out.

It wasn't his brother. It wasn't Gibbon and his side-kick. It wasn't Jean Louise . . .

'Course I'd like to see her again. Somehow it didn't seem right to me that she could look all that young and fresh after being married to Beecher Turnbull.

Then I figured that was what Red meant. The damned injun. He thought I was going into town just to see that pretty little whiskey-haired girl . . .

I woke at daybreak, smelling coffee and flapjacks. Not saying anything, I went out and washed my face, but didn't feel like scraping the stubble with cold water, nor did I want Turnbull to think I was getting duded up for his benefit.

"Bring back some dried fruit, apricots if there is any," Red said as I climbed aboard old Buck. "And try not to be late for supper."

"You got any more dumb injun jokes?" I asked irritably.

"No," he said.

One man travels faster'n two. I wasn't paying attention or wasting time on grading the condition of the forage, the weather, or the variety of loose animals scattered over the broad Juniper Valley floor, nor did I take time to stop along the way for a drink of water at one of the little ranchsteads that were mostly abandoned by their old owners and barely maintained by Beecher Turnbull, who'd taken them over.

My first stop was Aufdemburg's Mercantile. The town in midweek was hardly stirring. A dog slept in the middle of the street and Marshal Witherspoon leaned back in his chair in front of the jail. Fly Swinner was standing at the edge of the boardwalk in front of the Prince Albert saloon, waiting for someone to buy him a drink. Frank Pedragal came from the other way with his big-wheeled wagon half full of wooden crates. Wade Filson had the hind foot of a workhorse between his legs, trimming the hoof.

I tied Buck to the rail next to a couple Tee-Bar broomtails, and went inside.

As always there was the minute it took to get my eyes used to the dim light.

Down at the end of the counter where Aufdemburg racked his rifles and six-guns, Dee Gibbon and his sidekick, Luis Huerta, were looking over a new Colt revolver fresh out of the box.

Aufdemburg was saying, "Ya, it's better than the .38 Lightning."

"I dunno," Gibbon objected. "Neither one of them is as smooth as the Frontier. Better they stick to what they know best."

Looking up, he handed the new revolver to me. "You're supposed to be a gunfighter—what do you think?"

The new double-action Colt .41 had a hard black rubber bird's-head grip, and it looked too complicated for country work.

"I don't need it," I said, handing it back.

"What do you need?" Aufdemburg asked.

"You carry any .38-55 Winchester cartridges?"

"Sure, I got a box, but they're a special order," Aufdemburg said, looking through the cartons of ammunition.

"Who are they for?"

"Mr. Turnbull."

"What are you diggin' for, Bengard?" Dee Gibbon growled, perking up and trying to look mean.

I damned near laughed at the runt in his extra-high-heeled boots and big hat, but then I remembered that some little ones have more they want to prove.

Gibbon without his boots would have stood about five and a half feet tall, and weighed about one sixty. One of his eyes was off line just enough to make an honest man worry, and his grainy skin had a muddy cast to it that made you think of skinned liver. Each of his buckteeth had two side-by-side tiny holes drilled in them. Ace Dietjen thought they had something to do with Apache Indians, but he couldn't really say, and Doc Meredith guessed they'd been drilled and filled up with some concoction by a snake oil salesman who promised it would add a foot on Gibbon's height. Something like that was probably true because Gibbon never said anything about those little holes in his teeth.

Luis Huerta, a Mexican, taller and thinner than Gibbon, started sidling to his right as soon as his partner's tone of voice changed.

"I reckon that's between me and Turnbull." I backed off a step so as to keep Huerta in my view.

"Now, boys, don't start nothin'," Aufdemburg said.

"You borrow Turnbull's long Winchester once in a while, Gibbon?" I said it straight out, feeling just mad enough to blow a hole through him and Huerta both, so like a couple of slimy maggots they looked.

"Why would I?" His eyes changed. He could see I was ready to cut loose my wolf.

"Yes or no?" I didn't fool around letting my hand dangle down my leg. I wrapped it around the walnut butt of my Peacemaker so there would be no mistakes.

"'Course I do once in a while." He tried to make it sound gruff and tough but it sounded like whining to me.

Huerta kept sidling off to the right and I was tired of backin' up.

"Get back over here with your partner, *cabrón,*" I said, flicking a glance at him. "I'm done dancin' to your tune."

His eyes went hard when I called him a sonofabitch, but he shrugged and lifted his hands in a gesture of defeat and sidled back again to where I could shoot him if I wanted.

"We don't say nothin'," Huerta said.

"Shut up," I said, and tried to find Gibbon's squint eye again. "Gibbon, I been hearin' about you scarin' my neighbors and it's upsettin' my temper."

"Now, boys—" Aufdemburg said again.

"It's not true," Gibbon said slowly, deciding I wouldn't try a shooting match here and now.

"I'm sayin' I don't want to hear no more of it or I'm goin' to tie a can to your tail."

"You talk a lot for a raggedy-ass horse thief." Gibbon smiled and showed those four little holes in a row across his yellow buckteeth. "Why don't you come outside and back up your big mouth?"

Made me mad all of a sudden, but I didn't want to break my hand again.

I lifted my hands clear to give him a fair chance, and he smiled bigger'n ever, then I dropped the right hand to the Colt, drew, pivoted on my left foot, and hit him across the mouth. The seven-inch barrel knocked him backwards. I was aiming straight at the Mexican's brisket all at the same time.

Huerta backed up, his face frozen and pearly. He lifted his hands and kept backing up until he was alongside Gibbon, who had both hands over his mouth.

Suddenly I cooled off and felt disappointed in myself. A man can let his temper dig his grave for him and here I was acting like a fool kid instead of a well-brought-up hombre who ought to know better.

"Get out of here," I said. "If I ever catch you carryin' a long rifle, I'll stick it up your ass sideways."

Gibbon wiped the blood off his mouth with the back of his hand. His drilled front teeth were bent in some now, but likely he could straighten them back out again.

"There's other days," Gibbon mumbled over his shoulder as they went out the front door.

"Mr. Bengard," Aufdemburg said when they'd gone, "I vish you vould not do such things in my store."

"You ought to keep polecats like that out."

"It's a free country," he protested weakly.

The team bells jingled on the door, and Aufdemburg moved toward the front of the store, glad to have a reason to get clear of me. I leaned over the counter and picked out the box of .38-55 cartridges and dropped them down inside a new rifle boot where they'd be lost for a while.

When I heard her voice, I knew I was in the soup. Deep down, maybe I'd come into town just for that, no matter the other provocation. Back in the caverns of the mind strange things go on that a man doesn't always control, and I'd suddenly caught myself wanting to hear that simple girlish lilt, wanting to taste and savor it, and feel the unbidden thrill in the special and secret sharing of it.

I moved toward the front of the store to see her better, wishing now I'd shaved.

She'd come in with young Dan Turnbull and they were looking at Aufdemburg's selection of gloves, which ran from fancy cotton to plain cowhide gauntlets.

She picked out a pair of gray kid gloves for Dan, laughing and teasing about how small his hands were, while I stayed back in the shadows watching her perfect oval face, free and innocent in its expression, her tumbling light brown hair tied into the frisky ponytail, the pale blue eyes merry and warm as she helped to fit the gloves onto his slender fingers.

There was the warmth all right, the outgoing, youthful warmth, but it wasn't for me, it was shining like a sun ray right across the young Dan.

"Wait, I really don't need gloves. After all, I can take care of myself—"

My heart sank when I saw the heedless desire in her, her dangerous intent whether she knew it or not, and her sure handling of him, whether he knew it or not.

Dan Turnbull was clearly enjoying himself, pretending to prefer the rough leather gauntlets of the working cowboy, smiling and chuckling at her whimsical nonsense, and old Aufdemburg was grinning like a jackass eating cactus as he looked from one to the other, seeing what I was seeing, but only thinking about what tasty gossip it would make, and not worrying about the doom that this cheery skylarking was challenging.

Satisfied with the gloves, they moved on back toward me to look at the linen handkerchieves which she seemed to think he needed.

Nearer, I could see his eyes were empty of guile, were happy and honest, but with a shadow of worry nonetheless passing over his thin features. I noticed too the rosy glow on his cheekbones like a fever had touched them, and I noticed his narrow chest as she lifted a shirt to his shoulders to check the fit.

I decided Red was right, as usual.

They saw me standing there like a blamed fool, and I could do nothing except touch my hat and say "Ma'am" and look her flush in her honest eyes and give a nod to the bright-faced young man.

Walking by them, I went on out the door feeling as if I'd been struck by a sledge hammer. The fair face, the true-blue eyes, the husky girlish laugh like double-forked lightning were powerful enough to set the world to wobbling.

I mounted Buck and rode across the street to the Prince Albert, stepped down, tied Buck, and went inside directly to the bar, not looking left or right.

"Whiskey," I said to Marvin Bohn, who was reaching for a beer stein.

He stared at me a second, then fetched a shot glass instead and put the bottle on the bar.

"Early, ain't it, for you?" He tilted up his derby, making talk.

"Early for what?"

"Never mind. I'm sorry I opened my mouth. Today's a day for twelve hours of silence in memory of all the bar dogs who ran off at the mouth and paid with their lives for it."

"That bad?" I murmured.

"You'll notice, my friend," he said in a quiet voice

with his head turned so no one could see him talking, "the big, broad man at the end of the bar. The handmade frock coat is lined with paisley silk. He smells of lavender, and he smokes oversized cigars. He owns half the Juniper country, has a big white house, a lovely child bride. You'd think such a big and important pasha would feel it unnecessary to bite the head off the barman who feeds him a free lunch, but, no, that is not the case."

"He find a fly in his drink?"

"No, it was a pair of beetles nesting in the free lunch."

"Some days go that way," I commiserated with him. "Seen Dee Gibbon?"

"In for one drink. Resembled a fat-lipped gopher. People looked at him too much and he left."

"Did he happen to talk to the big he-boar?"

"He did," Marvin Bohn said, then turned to face the bar, his private conversation finished.

"If I had the sense of a jaybird I'd get out of here," I said.

"Yes, but you don't and won't."

"Besides, I rode all this way to say my piece."

"I don't want no shootin' inside."

I poured another drink of forty rod and watched the room in the mirror. This early in the day no one was playing cards, and, except for Fly Swinner and Dutch Feldcamp leaning at the other end of the bar, there was only Beecher Turnbull and a kid that he kept around to run errands he'd nicknamed Shuffle from the way he dragged his feet.

Turnbull faced the mirror, concentrating on reading some kind of a legal document and sipping his brandy.

It was my play. I'd come into town to say my piece to him, and now I couldn't figure out how to get his attention.

Without tasting my drink, I went out and fetched my bullet-torn shirt from my saddlebag, came back in, and this time aimed directly at Beecher Turnbull's back.

The kid, Shuffle, mumbled and Turnbull jerked away

from the paper he was reading and looked over his shoulder at me.

"Bengard?" He was quick. One second he was deep in the document, the next second he'd turned with his hands ready for anything.

"Turnbull—" I laid the folded-up shirt on top of his legal document.

"What the hell . . . ?" he muttered, never taking his eyes off mine.

I was trying to see his face, his hands, and how his feet were planted all at the same time.

"That shirt has a bullet-torn collar on it," I said stiffly. "I reckon it was a .38-55 rifle that did it."

"How do you reckon?" he asked softly, his big hands bulging and forming into fists.

I took the brass casing from my breast pocket and flipped it onto the bar.

"So?"

"So it fits your rifle." I took half a step to the right in case he was set to throw that bulging right hand. My hand was in easy reach of my .44.

"There's thousands of those rifles."

"You sayin' it wasn't yours?"

"I'm tellin' you to stay off my range."

"Mister, if I'm in your house, robbin' your goods, you got a right to shoot me. But if I'm riding public range, the first chickenshit backshooter that tries me is goin' to die my way."

Watching his wide, beefy face, I could still see his right boot move forward and his balance shift on the toe of his left foot, setting up for that lunge and right haymaker. He was very fast for a big man. His eyes were right on mine, cool, contemptuous, and then he made his shift, pivoting and lunging forward with the massive right fist winging in.

If I hadn't seen how he did it on Bud Mabry, I'd have been knocked from hell to breakfast by that mule-shoe right hand, but when his feet told me to move, I started my own left with my shoulder behind it, and shifted slightly forward and to my right so that his right-hand sucker punch whistled by my ear and his oncoming jaw collided with my own short, left hook. My hand felt as if it had cracked a granite headstone, but it tagged him perfectly on the edge of his jaw, and his head bounced back on his thick neck, and his eyes rolled up.

I moved aside as he continued his trajectory and plowed the sawdust, facedown. He didn't move except for a reflexive twitching of his splayed-out fingers.

I walked back to my place at the bar, finished my drink, and dug in my pocket for a coin, when Marvin Bohn said, "On the house. Is he alive?"

"So far."

"Sounded like you hit him with a board, Wes. How's your hand?" Fly Swinner came over like a sympathetic old sidekick and licked his dry lips.

"It'll do."

I went out to the hitch rail, swung up on Buck, and took the trail out, feeling better.

I tried to think of why I should get so riled up and shove myself into the middle of a ruckus. Most times I'd have tried tracking the dry-gulcher or asking quiet questions, easing along like I was a piece of the scenery until I was damned positive about who it was that had pulled the trigger on a .38-55 rifle. Then I would have pulled him out of the herd and either killed him or cut his hand off, depending on how I felt at the time.

It wasn't like me—good old Wes Bengard, the quiet cowboy—to pick a fight with a dunghill banty rooster, a fight I knew I could win. Why would I do such a thing as that? If Dee Gibbon was my bushwhacker, I should have taken the time to prove it beyond any doubt, and then put him down forever.

Do it to his boss, too. Except for his being a blowhard talking about all his range and his property, there was no reason to pick a fight with him before I had better evidence than a single brass casing.

The truth is you set him up for your left hook, I told myself, trying to be as honest as I could.

So what's this all about, Wesley Bengard? How come you're actin' like a rosy-assed orangutan all of a sudden?

Then I had the momentary vision of the fresh, friendly face, the direct blue eyes, the childlike ponytail . . .

I had to admit that all I'd been doing was working off steam. What I was really madder'n hell about was that this beautiful, innocent girl had married a turd like Beecher Turnbull, and now was turning her attention on to the kid brother.

And she didn't know me from Adam's off ox!

"Ya damn fool!" I said out loud, and Buck picked up his ears like I was cussin' him.

I came into the ranch whistling, and after putting Buck in the barn with a scoop of oats, ambled over to the corral where Red was taking turns playing the sack on a couple of broncs.

"One at a time ain't fast enough?" I asked.

"I'm thinkin' about startin' a factory. A big brick building with a lot of belts and pulleys throwin' sacks and ropes around, then we push a thousand horses a day through that building, and they come out at the other end two by two, quiet as a treeful of apples."

"Poor feller, I reckon you been alone so long the prairie wind done wore your mind down."

"Did you bring my dried apricots?"

I set my jaw and said nothing, I was so mad at myself.

"Likely the prairie wind or something of like value wore your thinker down some," he murmured.

"Likely," I said, owning up to my mistake. "I was right there and set to give my order, but somethin' came up and I plumb forgot it."

"Important?"

"Wasn't nothin'. Just human beings."

"The shock was too much for you," he nodded. "I guess next time I'll tie a note to Beau and send him to town."

71

"You don't know but what he might be an irresponsible drinkin' mule, given the chance."

He went on inside and fired up the stove while I finished sacking the pair of wild ones. They'd turn out to be first-rate cow ponies the way they were learning their early lessons. A long ways from being bitted and trained to split-second reining, but they were well started.

I wished they were ready to sell. I was feeling a big urge to get out of the flea-bit Juniper country and settle down where the señoritas rocked your hammock under the banana tree and brought you a cold beer whenever you patted one on the butt.

We spent a solid week working together from daybreak 'til dark, taming and training the geldings and mares and fillies.

We weren't in such a hurry that we skipped any time on any of the twenty-eight head. Some big ranchers, that don't give a damn about the horse or the man, will hire a buckaroo to slap a saddle on a bronc's back, then lift the blindfold and let the two of them fight it out. It don't make much of a nevermind to the rancher; he can replace either one of them. He gives the buckaroo ten dollars to ride the bronco, next day a plain old cowpoke has to try to ride that same horse to work and finish breaking him for nothing.

We did it different. Our horses didn't have any buck in them nor any other bad habits when we put them up for sale.

Sometimes a rogue or two can't be broke and we slough them off onto Ace Dietjen on the condition he doesn't mention our names in connection with the horse.

Along with our ideas on breaking the wild ones, we'd culled our ranch studs until we had what looked to be a cross between an Arab, a Morgan, and a Hambletonian, with a touch of Standardbred, an honest-to-God all-around type of a horse.

We'd picked out half a dozen mares with the same general conformation. They wore our brand and we kept them fairly close by giving them a bait of grain once in a while.

Both Red and I took quite a bit of pride in changing the wild broncs into well-mannered cow ponies, and we never worried that we'd cheated somebody, or sent out a mankiller who'd throw himself over backwards when you weren't expecting trouble, or a biter who would savage a dog or an old widderwoman if they got close enough.

It wasn't a bad life or I guess we'd have changed it to be better. We didn't have a boss like Beecher Turnbull raggin' us, or a banker like Mex Abrams taking our profit, and we weren't afraid of any of our customers coming after us with a goosegun.

Maybe it was some lonesome out there, but there wasn't any female naggin' and whenever worse came to worse, there was always Thelma Parker.

Our wild ones were all pretty much tamed down except for one ordinary-looking bay gelding who trained well enough, except he was clumsy and sometimes fell where other horses didn't.

"He has the mark of the goat," Red had said, pointing at the worn spots on his knees. "You can't train that out of him and we don't want to sell anybody a horse with that mark."

"You want to turn him back on the range, shoot him, or sell him to Ace Dietjen?"

"We've got a lot of work in him. If Ace sells him, the buyer will be expecting trouble."

"Is he dangerous?"

"More dangerous to himself. He'll crack a knee someday and he'll go to the glue factory."

I worked some extra with the bay with the mark of the goat because it was about time for Ace Dietjen to turn up, and I wanted to have the gelding bitted and reined beforehand. He had no buck in him or other bad habits that we knew of, just his clumsiness, which we couldn't fix.

I rode him out on the range where our little herd of cattle grazed and tried to see if he could cut out a steer, but sure enough, on his first quick move, he fell. Halfway expecting it, I made a roll over his shoulder and missed landing in a patch of creeping devil cactus by an inch. I hung on to the reins in my swan dive so I didn't have to walk home.

When Ace Dietjen arrived a few days later in midmorning without a cloud in the sky and the northwest whining its miserable, inhuman dirge, we were mighty glad for his company.

Red made a fresh pot of coffee and put out some cinnamon buns left over from breakfast, and we sat around the table catching up on the news.

Not that there was so much of it, with Juniper Valley not quite as populated as the Sonoran desert or the Humboldt Sink, but we always enjoyed Ace's yarns whether they were true or not.

". . . you know, some time ago I was back in Arkansas, mostly because I'd never been there before, and I had a string of no-good mules and burros. I passed through a little village, but no one was interested in my stock.

"'What's the matter, you folks don't like my stock?' I asked an old-timer friendly-like.

"'Stranger,' he said to me, 'everybody in Arkansas knows if a mule or a burro don't carry his tail high, well, he can't never pull his own weight!'

"So I drove on up the trail until I come in sight of another little backwater, looked through my herbs and drugs, then I shoved a piece of gingerroot up the ass of every critter I had.

"I tell you, when we come into that little town, those mules and burros were carrying their tails high as flags on the Fourth of July. Traded off every one of them for low-tail mules, and got about three dollars to boot on each one. Then I turned back and went to the first little hamlet, freshened up those worthless mules with a piece of ginger up their backsides, and that old man said, 'Well, son, I see you've got some good Arkansas mules this time,' and he bought all eight of them and threw in a jug of his blackberry moonshine to boot."

"Gingerroot," Red said, almost smiling.

"Well, if you're short on gingerroot, you can swab his bung with carbolic acid and he'll put his tail up for you, don't worry," Ace said with a grin.

"I might try that on Red's mule, if I could get within six feet of him and had him hog-tied," I said.

"I see that the scab on Beecher Turnbull's nose came off all right and he's lookin' ornerier'n ever."

"No offense, but how'd he get a scab on his nose?" Red asked. "Come from tryin' to sweep the floor of the Prince Albert with his face?"

Ace glanced at me and I looked off at the lamp on the top of the stove.

"I seen his left hand was swolled up," Red said. "He's got weak hands."

"And a weak brain," I said.

"They say things are gettin' kind of tight in the big house," Ace said, covering up his mistake. "They say little brother Dan is more housebound than ever."

"Sick a lot?" I asked.

"They had Doc Meredith up there a few times, but it don't help."

"What'd he say was the matter with the kid?" Red asked.

"He don't say. He starts lookin' everywhere but at you, and then he'll say maybe it's pleurisy, maybe it's the heaves, maybe he's bull-windy, but it's always a maybe."

"I knew an injun once that died from the maybes," Red said.

"He seems to be strong enough to walk and get about some, but Beecher is ridin' alone a lot. 'Course, folks will talk about a thing like that.

"Like a young man and a young lady stayin' upstairs all day long, no matter how many times the cook calls 'em to dinner," Ace said.

"Who's the cook?" Red asked.

"Metta Snapp. She ain't much of a cook," said Ace, "but she'd make a hell of a bulldogger."

"I reckon Beecher wanted a bulldogger in the house more'n a cook."

"That seems to be the general feeling in Buttonwillow," Ace said with a nod. "For sure Beecher is carryin' a heavy load, with the carpetbags under his eyes lookin' like black-and-blue blisters, and lowering his head down like a bull with glanders."

"Glanders?"

"Lump jaw then, like he had a multiple toothache."

"He get that from sweepin' the floor with his face?" Red asked.

"No. It's just come on lately. It's somethin' inside his head that don't agree with him. Sometimes it brings him in early from the ranch and he goes right upstairs to rest."

"I'd guess that's some worse'n TB," I said.

"Might even be contagious. It appears to me that Jean Louise has caught a mild case of it, and brother Dan has some symptoms, too."

"Mrs. Snapp got it too?" Red asked.

"Not yet. Mrs. Snapp, of course, is a hoss that's never been rode, and the only thing she ever caught was her ear in a keyhole."

"Times I can see the beauty of this forlorn place," I said, shaking my head in a kind of pity for other folks' problems.

"You ain't seen Dee Gibbon about, have you?" Ace asked, getting off the subject of the Turnbull family.

"We're not expectin' him," I said.

"Wes told me," Red said to encourage Ace.

"Then you know Dee is giving Doc Meredith a lot of dental practicin'."

"I told Red because I figured the sonofabitch will be settin' up a long-range shootin' stand right soon."

"You figure him for the bushwhackin'?"

"It's both ways, I think."

"How?"

"Gibbon's usin' Turnbull's rifle and he's on Turnbull's payroll."

"Likely." Ace nodded thoughtfully. "But then Dee can do a little work on the side, too, even if he isn't told to do it."

"That's why one of us ride a circle around the place every mornin' at daybreak," Red said.

"And out on the range we stay spread out," I added. "And I'm damned glad I bent the runt's teeth in."

"Well, everyone knows Turnbull's in the clear. He was gettin' his hair cut and talkin' to Marshal Witherspoon most of Monday last week when the Salkeld kid was bushwhacked."

"Salty's son?"

"No doubt he was rustlin' a few beeves off the Tee-Bar," Ace said, nodding. "They found some Tee-Bar branded hides in his camp, and he was sellin' beef off his wagon."

"Damn fool kid . . ." I said.

I knew him a little. Not much brighter than his pa, he was all right so long as he had a home and something to eat. But with the ranch sold and the old man drunk, he had no place to go.

"I'm for hangin' rustlers," Red said.

"Sure, anybody is," Ace said, "but dry-gulchin' ain't the same thing. A man with a long rifle don't make up much of a jury."

"What's the good news?" I asked.

"The good news is Thelma Parker married Dad Crawford and they're expectin' their first in about four months."

"Kind of soon, ain't it?" Red asked.

"Not too soon for Thelma." Ace smiled.

"Hell, I was plannin' on goin' to town next week," I said. "Anything else?"

"Reminds me of the time I got slickered with a dummy horse that would push when you wanted him to back, and lay down when you wanted him to prance around, wouldn't eat, and looked poor, although he'd looked shiny and full of beans when I traded for him. Was another horse trader over at Carson I owed a trick to. On the way I stopped in at Aufdemburg's Mercantile and bought a dollar's worth of cocaine and just before I come into Carson I put a pinch of it back on the tonsils of my dummy horse.

"Oh, he perked right up, and in a short while I made a deal with my old friend and went away with a profit. Next day I went back and the dummy horse looked as bad as ever.

"'Got a sick horse here,' the other trader said. 'I never seen anything like it'.

"'It's a new type of colic,' I said. 'The only cure is to soap him.'

"So that meant he had to give that big horse a soap enema, which he did, and whilst he was getting all messed up at the horse's hind end, I went up to the front and give the horse another pinch of cocaine on his tonsils, and don't you know, he perked right up!"

Ace's dark, foxy face shone with the joy of accomplishment.

"'I guess you know how to cure him,' I said to my old friend as I was leaving'. 'Every time he gets down a little, you can just soap him up again.'"

We laughed at Ace's yarn and cleared the Juniper Valley trouble out of our minds.

Whilst Ace went on talking, Red made prune cake,

fried some salt pork, put in some sauerkraut from the keg, and heated up some Mexican beans to go with his sourdough bread, and we ate a pretty good supper.

Next morning I showed Ace the bay horse and he looked at the spots on his knees and shook his head.

"I'll have to keep him stalled 'til the hair grows back and then dye his knees. It ain't hardly worth it."

"If you don't take him for ten dollars, I'm goin' to shoot him for hog feed," Red said.

"I'll give you the ten dollars if you throw in the rest of that prune cake to boot," Ace said, not cracking a smile.

6

OF THE TWENTY-SEVEN WILD ONES IN THE CORRAL, WE saved back three good brood mares in foal, probably to the big Tee-Bar stud, and put them out with our small remuda of well-bred and well-mannered breeders.

The two dozen left were still a little salty, but none of them were marked up or contrary minded. Red's patience and care showed. By the end of August we had ridden each one of them many miles and were confident they were top horses, worth top price.

On the morning of August twenty-fourth, Red packed Beau with our traveling gear. We mounted up, turned our cavvy out, and commenced driving them up the northwest trail toward Carson, more than a hundred miles away.

Up on old Buck, I felt a kind of sadness to be taking this band of good horses off to a strange place where they'd be bought by strange men who might be good or bad to them. I'd gotten kind of a paternal feeling about these horses, which it seemed we'd raised up from unruly children to responsible citizens of the horse nation. The prouder I felt about them, the more I hated to send them out into the world.

Still, we weren't in the business of collecting horses, the way the Plains Indians did: our business was training and selling. So the pintos, the sorrels, the bays, and the roans, the blacks and the grays, the buckskins and the chestnuts with their stars and stockings, snips and blazes, were on their way to market as if they were no more than a herd of steers.

The grass was better as we approached the mountains and I bought a little grain wherever there was a settlement, because we wanted them to show well when we put them in the sales yard.

They sure were a pretty sight pacing along with the wind in their manes, all full of power and confidence, sometimes playing tag, or being bossy, sometimes just cavorting over the flatland for the fun of feeling free.

"Damned hammerheads," I said to Red as we rode along behind them. "Probably break their damn necks foolin' around like that."

"Give them a few days of fun," he said. "They'll never have it so fine as right now."

We found grassy camps and good water when we commenced skirting the mountains, turning north. Red had packed a cast-iron spider along and if there was time left over after hobbling the herd, he'd set it on the coals, put a pie inside, and then heap the coals on the flat lid. About the time we were ready for the soogan, the coals would be gone, and we'd have a piece of apple and raisin pie, and eat the rest of it for breakfast.

"Feels good to have the backshootin' worry behind us," I said one evening, watching the coals on the top of the spider change colors and slowly turn to ash.

"It's still there, last I heard," Red said, mixing flour and baking powder, lard and salt together for the morning's biscuits.

"Likely Dee Gibbon will get himself killed before too long. Folks is tired of blood fights over open range."

"They keep it up, the politicians will take the land and put it up for rent," Red muttered. "And you know who can pay rent."

"We don't need to fight for it," I said. "We don't have anybody to leave it to, even if we could keep it."

"What am I doin' it for then?" Red murmured.

"Damn if I know. Maybe it's hope that a good woman will come along and give you a family to work for."

"Maybe I'll bring back one of them bouncy Mexican ladies from San Blas," he said.

"Them bouncy ones get to swellin' up after a time."

"Them tall, thin ones are meaner'n hell, though," he said, as if he'd been studying the matter. "Maybe by the time they lard up to be barrel size, they'll try harder to please you."

"You can't win." I shook my head. "Them round ones can't move fast enough to please a man. It takes a lean dog for the long race."

Even while we were talking, the memory of the whiskey-haired girl would flash through my mind to deny any dream I might have of a bouncy little Mexican lady. It was like Jean Louise was saying, "Go ahead and play your games, but you're roped, forefooted, and hog-tied forevermore by the lady that ought to be by your side."

"Oh, hell," I said, "I'm goin' to turn in."

"Don't want any pie?" Red's tone was mild and yet commiserating, as if he knew what was going on in my head and wished he could do something about it.

"In the mornin'. It'll be better cold," I said, and moved to my bedroll outside the firelight and tried to dream about the dark, bouncy ones, but it didn't work.

I dream of Jeanie with the light brown hair . . .

In the morning I felt better after a double ration of pie and a couple biscuits besides, and you couldn't beat the fine weather and the wild mountains on our left that made us smaller than mites on a flea's belly button. The grandness of that country put me to thinking about moving the ranch on over here when we'd squirreled away a little money.

"No mustangs left," Red said when I mentioned the idea.

"We could bring our own remuda and a couple of bunches of wild ones to add in."

"Possible . . ." He nodded after a while. "More water, more grass over here."

"Back in one of these canyons there has to be an old abandoned ranchstead belly-deep in grass," I said as we rode along.

We couldn't take time to look up every valley that opened up into the plain, but it was pleasant to think about such a place. Still, with Beecher Turnbull and Huerta and Gibbon roaming around back home, seeing how easy it would be to plunder our remuda and burn down the ranch, we felt some anxious to get on back.

The cavvy was in top condition when we crossed the river into Carson and drove them down a back street to the sales pens near the railroad freight yards.

A man in a black suit with a cigar stuck in the side of his mouth heard us coming and had the gate already open. Our band trotted inside like good students ready to graduate.

"Klaus Koberman," he said, shaking hands and offering us each a cigar. "Pretty fair bunch of mustangs."

"They're reined and ready to ride," Red said.

"You want me to buy 'em all, or do you want to pay the percentage to auction them off next Saturday?"

"Depends on your price," I said, and we fell into dickering, leaning against the high plank corral while the horses drank and snuffled at the ground.

He gave us a price for all twenty-four of them, and then he said, "You never know what you'll get at auction. Sometimes it's more, sometimes less."

"I reckon we'd like to go get a room and a bath and then come back and talk with you."

"Fine. You ask around and you'll find my offer is as good as you'll get."

We went over to the barbershop and got ourselves shaved and sheared and took a bath in the bathhouse, then went over to the Palace Hotel and hired a room.

It was time to eat, but first we went over to a haberdashery and bought new sets of clothes, so that we could go into the restaurant without feeling like a couple chancred outlaws.

Red ordered the baked Maryland chicken and I asked for the sweetbreads and oyster pie, something I'd never tried before, and I must say, it even beat Red's marrow-gut stew.

Stockmen we met, we asked about the going price for a good riding horse, and when we rode back to Koberman's sales yard, we saw a couple young Paiutes riding the horses bareback. They were being a mite cautious with them, wary of being bit or kicked or throwed.

Red went over and talked to them a while in Paiute, then came back over where I was setting on the top rail watching.

"They said so far they're well mannered," Red said, climbing up beside me. "And I told them they were all the same."

Old Koberman slouched out of his office, chewing on his short cigar, and beckoned one of the riders over. He talked a while and then climbed up next to me.

"Tell me true," he said, "you got any ringboned ringers in that bunch?"

"Mr. Koberman, our business is raising and selling a good horse. We're building up a rep for top-quality animals, and we can't afford to slip in any stump-suckers. Every one of them is guaranteed sound and broke to ride."

"Whereabouts you boys from?" he nodded, not believing a word I said.

"Juniper Valley country," Red said.

"Out there by Buttonwillow," Koberman said, knowing the country. "You see any of that bushwhackin' we hear so much about over here?"

"I had a shirt tore up," I nodded, "but it's likely all over now."

He pulled out an envelope from inside his coat and on the back of it he had colors and numbers written down in a column and a total at the bottom. "As I see it, your best horse is the big blue roan. The boy says he's gentle as a kitten and rides well. He's likely a five-hundred-dollar horse. The others vary some, that calico being the cheapest because he's small and got a hammerhead. Still, he's worth a hundred dollars. Add up my figures, you get forty-two hundred on the choppin' block right now. Or I'll run them through auction for you and take my ten percent out of the total."

"I'd as liefer sell 'em right now, but from what I hear, maybe they'll bring up to six thousand," I said.

We all knew what we were doing and as the Indian boys rode around the big corral on the bright, healthy horses, we came to an agreement of five thousand two hundred, which was considerable more than we'd expected when we left the ranch.

"Your brands are good," he said as we went in his office. "There ain't any scars or rope burns on 'em. Tell you the truth, boys, I never saw such a perfect band of mustangs before."

"We'll bring you in some more next spring," I said, "so long as it's worth our time."

"And gettin' shot at!" he chuckled, counting out 260 double eagles in stacks of tens. When Red and I nodded agreement on the tally, he swept the pile of gold into a leather poke and handed it over to me.

"Don't drink it up, boys," he said. "You can do wonders with that much cash money."

We shook hands, rode over to a livery near the hotel, and put up the horses and the mule, then went into the hotel, carrying the heavy sack of gold pieces.

"What do you say?" I asked.

"We already got our clothes," Red said, looking at me. "A woman can't be more'n three dollars."

"Say a hundred apiece, then."

"Sure."

I dug out five gold pieces and so did he, then we went over to the desk and asked the hotel manager to keep the bag in his safe.

I quit worrying about the money as soon as he clanged the door shut and pushed over a receipt.

"You boys lookin' for a decent place to drink, we've got a nice bar in the hotel," he said, smiling nice and shiny at us.

"Thanks," I said, not explaining that we didn't want to drink in a decent place, we wanted to drink in an indecent place.

During the late afternoon and the long night, we found quite a few such bars to drink in, and had a couple good fights with hombres that thought brass knucks and lead-shot saps was something new for the country boys. Sure enough, along the way the indecent women arrived, the flossies in bangles and bows, with big eyes and husky voices, and old Red and I were so happy and full of love for the whole world, we couldn't resist sharin' with the troopers.

Once in a while we'd see a lawman off through the cigar smoke, but we didn't land in jail, we didn't get beat up or shanghaied, we didn't fall down and pass out on the floor, we didn't get overly shortchanged, but we did do a lot of drinking and eating, dancing and hooting and hollering, and we woke up in a rooming house that smelled bad enough to puke a skunk, found our pockets empty, left the weary doxies, our eyes downcast, and back at the hotel, went back to bed again.

That was the hundred-dollar night, and once we were started back down the trail, I laughed and giggled, remembering snatches of it, and I reckoned it was worth every penny.

Red looked a little cobby at first, his greenish color resembling that of rotten pig liver, and he stopped in a hurry once and went into the brush, where he retched and belched and groaned a while. When he come back out, he had tears in his eyes but his color was better.

That night we ate some buttered white bread we'd bought in Carson and went to bed without even building a fire.

We traveled faster without our band of horses and even Beau was willing to give a little extra because he knew he was going back home to lay around the rest of the year.

I thought some about that five thousand dollars we had. Of course it was only half mine, but Red might loan me a good chunk of it if I happened to need it to impress the whiskey-haired girl that I could take care of her all right. Then I saw how foolish my thoughts were running, and resolved to squirrel most of it away, maybe each of us take a thousand dollars and ride for Mexico come first snow. In the spring we could take a *pasear* back here to the foot of the mountains and find a little valley with a stream running down the middle of it.

We rode into Buttonwillow three days after leaving Carson, which made it the fifth day of September. There was a little sharpness of autumn in the air, but out here where trees were about as scarce as birdshit in a cuckoo clock, it hardly showed that summer was over and winter on its way.

The town was just as bedraggled and dusty, warped and lonely as ever.

We swung down in front of the Prince Albert and went into the cool darkness, just about tiptoeing it was so quiet and mournful inside.

After my eyes adjusted to the gloom, I recognized Marvin Bohn, lean, sardonic, enduring in his white sack apron and derby hat.

"Wesley, Red," he said, "You're looking prosperous, what'll you have?"

"Beer," I said, and Red shook his head.

Marvin drew the beer into a mug and set it front of me, saying, "Been off somewheres?"

"Sold our stock in Carson," I said.

"Get a good price?"

"Pretty country over there." I lifted the beer and nodded.

Now I could see the men idling at the bar and the four playing poker at the round table.

As usual Fly Swinner was propped down at the end talking to Dag Petersen and Dutch Feldcamp. I wondered what they could have to talk about. Losses, likely.

Midway stood Bolivar Cromwell, the pigeon-breasted lawyer sporting a fancy gray suit that matched his curly gray hair. Next to him stood E. Mickelsen Abrams, the fox-faced banker we called Mexican, and Jacob Levy, the haberdasher. They'd all glanced our way when we came in, sized us up, and now were looking somewhere else.

Next to me Wayne Farnhorst, the harness maker, was pooching his mouth in and out like bellows and staring up at the lady in the brass bed. Doc Meredith, Ed Lewis, Frank Pedragal, and Ace Dietjen were playing five-card stud and down the other way, Dee Gibbon and Luis Huerta kept to themselves.

"Holiday today?" I asked into the quietness. "Or somebody die?"

"I guess you haven't heard," Farnhorst said between pooching his mouth in and out.

"No. Reckon not."

"I reckon I'm talkin' too much," he said, staring up at the naked lady again and pooching away.

I looked at Marvin Bohn, but he'd picked up a glass to shine and was offering nothing.

Mex Abrams turned toward me and said in that nasal, contemptuous lingo he used, "It's nothing really. It seems that Jean Louise Turnbull and young Dan Turnbull have departed without saying adieu."

My tongue stuck, and I probably blinked. I felt Red's elbow pushing up against mine.

"Where'd they go?" I tried to hold my tone steady.

"They did not deem it worthy of their dignity to impart the itinerary or their destination."

"Turnbull?" I asked Melvin Bohn directly.

"I've heard he's still in the big house," Marvin said quietly, "but he's not too busy."

"Drunk as a fiddler's clerk," Mex Abrams said. "What can we do to help our friend?"

I never knew Mex Abrams to help anybody except relieve them of their money, property, and baggage.

"I reckon you could take over his business before some outsider scamp gets the idea," I said, then I cooled off as I felt Red's elbow give me another little jab.

"We got work to do, Nez," Red said quietly.

"The goddamned sneakin' little sonofabitch," Gibbon said sharply to himself, or the whole room, it didn't make any difference.

"How do you know if you didn't see them go?" I asked the men at the poker table.

Ace glanced up at me, tossed a chip into the pot, looked back up, and said, "Big Metta Snapp seen the empty rooms, seen Beech wandering around like a poleaxed billy goat with a bottle of Old Blackbird in his hand."

"Did they take the buggy?" I could hardly believe it.

"I doubt if anyone's thought to look," Jacob Levy said quickly. "It's a good question."

"Well, we don't have a train or a stage, and I doubt if they walked," Bolivar Cromwell boomed out like he was addressing an audience that was hard of hearing.

"They couldn't take the buggy," Wayne Farnhorst murmured. "I'm mendin' the harness. Got a broken hame . . ."

"Lovebirds fly," Frank Pedragal sang out in a high-pitched voice.

"They had to take the buggy," Doc Meredith said. "Dan Turnbull's too sick to go any other way."

"And Beecher Turnbull didn't jump on a horse and

run them down?" I asked, still finding the event too wild to believe.

"It ain't right," Farnhorst said to the woman in the brass bed. "It ain't right."

"I heard a lot of racket over there a couple nights ago," Ed Lewis said.

A small, spare man with faded hair and eyebrows, Lewis and his wife rented rooms to occasional travelers. Ed was too old a man to be out prowling at night, but sometimes people saw him, or somebody a lot like him, sneaking around.

"What kind of racket?" Mex Abrams looked over at him.

"Yelling and hollering. Oh, they were carrying on something awful."

"What were they saying?" Bolivar Cromwell demanded.

"I couldn't hear exactly. Just a lot of bellering and caterwauling. Stuff breaking. You know—dishes and furniture."

I figured he was adding on extra now. Chances were he'd heard something, but he'd had to have been at the window to hear a dish break.

"It's been goin' on for weeks," Frank Pedragal said.

I looked at Red, nodded.

"Boots and saddles," he said.

I dropped a coin on the bar, and passing by the poker table, I said, "Let me know how it goes, Ace."

He looked up from his cards and nodded.

=== 7 ===

WOOD RATS HAD DISCOVERED WE WERE GONE AND MOVED into the cabin, availing themselves of all the comforts of home. They scattered when I opened the door, but the rattlesnakes who had the same idea as the rats weren't quite so quick. I broke a shovel handle on one and shot the other as he glided away, looking for a new rathole.

"Helluva note—" Red said, coming on the run after hearing the racket.

"I guess I left the window open," I said, looking around at the chewed-up cornshucks that had been my mattress, broken crocks and jars, and the ruin of the open shelves, where the rats had been eating the beans and dry cereals and anything else that would go down a rat's throat, including the baking powder, soap, and lamp wicks.

All that stuff had to go somewhere, and the rats had left a foot-deep layer of feathers, shavings, broken glass and pottery, and rat turds all over the floor, with centipedes and scorpions trying to hide in the knotholes.

"Another week and they'd have ate the whole cabin up," I grumbled.

"Let's start with the top shelves and work down," Red said, and commenced removing everything from the shelves and wiping them with a soapy rag.

Using the broken shovel, I started scooping the mess into an old washtub and carrying it out to the dump behind the barn, grumbling and cussing all the way and back.

"Helluva way for a man with money in his pocket to have to live. If the rats don't get you, the snakes will . . . If you'da had a woman to leave home we wouldn't have to be actin' like old-maid housekeepers . . ."

"It's just nature," Red said solidly. "Maybe you got something else aggravating your mind . . ."

"I got Mexico on my mind," I lied, and simmered down.

It took us until dark to sluice out the cabin, and all we had to eat was what we'd bought in Buttonwillow. I flattened out some tin airtights and nailed them over the ratholes.

"Red, put arsenic and strychnine on your list."

Without my cornshuck tick, the bunk was hard as soft pine lumber is, and in the morning there was no coffee.

"I kept the coffee beans in a jar on the top shelf," Red said. "They must've knocked it off and broke it."

"Next time we go somewhere I'm goin' to leave a couple of bobcats in here with nothing to eat."

"The snakes were tryin' to hold 'em down."

"Put a new shovel on the list," I growled.

Except for the damage in the cabin, the rest of the ranchstead was about normal. There was water for the cattle and horses, and enough dry grass to carry them through to spring. We didn't keep dogs or cats because we were gone so much, and except for a general dustiness and a collection of tumbleweeds blown up against the corral fence, nothing much had changed.

"We better take Beau to pack the grub home," Red

said. "He's been lookin' forward to several months' rest, but he'll have to wait some."

Coming into Buttonwillow, we passed the big two-story white house with the lookout on top. There was no one up there, naturally, which made the whole place seem extravagant and foolish and all the more empty.

I left Red at Aufdemburg's Mercantile and rode toward the Prince Albert, thinking none of it was any of my damned business.

Yet, no doubt about it, the vision of Jean Louise was in my mind, demure but frank, innocent but forthright, reserved but generous, free but trapped, beautiful but wasted. All I had for her was sympathy and an urge to help her out. I guess to say it straight, I would have been pleased to serve her any way she wanted.

But this kind of thinking wasn't taking in the plain facts, which was that she'd married the big man for some reason other than his sweet manners, and she'd run off with his brother, which I could understand easy enough. What I couldn't understand was the thin, mild-mannered consumptive having enough guts to carry her off.

If you looked at it that way, something didn't add up.

Better a cup of coffee and a piece of pie and some cheery company than the gloom of the Prince Albert, I decided, changing my mind. I turned Buck back across the street, and tied him up in front of Ed's Cafe.

Ed looked up, grinned, and hollered, "Well, look at the richest man west of Buttonwillow! Howdy, Wes, good to see you. Hear you cleaned out Carson!"

I nodded, feeling better already, and as I sat down, he called back into the kitchen, "Piece of cherry pie, Melba. I'll take care of the coffee."

"Now, then"—he turned back to me and put his face close to mine—"tell me, is it true they've got sporters over there that wear cowboy boots and carry blacksnake whips coiled up around their shoulders?"

"It's worse'n that, Ed," I whispered. "They got

sporters over there that use gopher snakes for garters and I don't know what else! I seen one that had his tail wrapped around her leg and his head was pokin' out of her bosom and ticklin' her under the chin."

"You don't say!" Ed pretended to believe me. "That's what's so nice about livin' in a small town, nothin' ever happens."

"I could only hold out one night in that awful place," I said. "It was such a sin swamp, it turned my stomach. Would you believe all they do over there is eat sweetbreads and oysters, drink Spanish brandy and French wines, and lay up with young ladies that giggle all the time?"

"Oh, I couldn't stand that!" Ed shook his head solemnly, then burst out with a hooting laugh. "By golly, Wes, I'm glad you survived the trip! Sure hope you didn't lose Red over there."

The cherry pie was perfect, the butter crust ready to melt in your mouth, and the coffee was fresh and better'n Red's most times.

My mood brightened considerable, and I was bragging some to Ed about how well our horses looked and how little trouble we had selling them, when in came Marshal Witherspoon and Mex Abrams, both talking fast and furious.

When they saw me they shut up.

They took seats at the table back in the corner and ordered coffee and doughnuts, which Ed served promptly, his peg leg clattering over the plank floor as he moved about, becoming now a top chop waiter instead of a jolly bullshooter.

I wasn't trying to listen in on that pair's table talk—in fact, I was so full up with mystery talk that was mostly frayed-out back fence gossip, I caught myself hurrying that delicious pie, and made myself slow down.

"But—" Witherspoon kept saying, "but—but . . ."

"They say . . ." Abrams persisted, "they say . . . they say . . . They say there was blood all over the carpet . . ."

"But—who says?" Witherspoon finally got it said.

"Metta Snapp," Abrams popped out, forgetting me and Ed.

"But—but . . . hell, she's been loco for—"

Ed winked at me as he pegged by with the coffeepot and I felt a knot in my stomach instead of the joyful presence of Melba's best baked goods.

I put a coin on the counter, murmured a thanks and so long, then drifted out the door before hearing any more.

I sure appreciate knowin' you, Wesley . . .

Wes, I told myself firmly, your business is horses. Keep your chin tucked under your collarbone and nobody will break your jaw.

I stood out on the boardwalk a while, chewing on a toothpick. I looked over at the mercantile, but Beau was still waiting for his pack. Nothing doing.

I took my time crossing over to the P.A., and even then waited a while, backing up to the wall, like I was resting up from the long walk, and trying to forget what I'd heard.

Blood all over the carpet!

No question Turnbull had a hot temper and big fists, and he could give anybody a bloody nose . . .

And the kid brother could be spitting up blood by now, it would be about time . . .

Or, hell, somebody could have cut himself on a knife or broken glass . . .

Had Turnbull got wind of their leaving? Or had they had a fight with him and then decided to leave?

Babe Silliman was sitting in at the poker game instead of Ace Dietjen; otherwise it looked the same as the day before. Fly Swinner, instead of leaning on the bar at the far end, was earning his space and maybe a couple drinks by sweeping the splintered floor, but Marvin Bohn stood as always like a blackjack oak fence post, his flat eyes hardly changing enough to acknowledge my arrival.

I had a sudden idea that a wild horse feels the way I did

just then when he smells the trap after he's already through the gate.

"A little beer," I said, coming up alongside Bud Mabry.

Marvin filled a glass and scraped off the suds with his finger before setting it in front of me.

"Howdy," Bud said, not looking my way.

The knot on his head was long gone, but his self-esteem hadn't returned.

"'Lo, Bud, how's the cattle business?"

"Feed's poor, except for locoweed."

"Price down, too?" I asked, just to be mean.

"Low enough to keep a small rancher broke."

"Hear about the empty barrel of flour?"

"No," Bud Mabry growled, preferring to be sour.

"Nothin' in it," I said, and seeing Wade Filson over on my right, I said, "Tell me the news, Wade?"

"Nothin' much goin' on," the long-waisted blacksmith said, his big curly beard showing spots where flying metal or sparks from his forge had burnt little holes. "I guess you heard your dream girl run off with a man?"

"What dream girl would that be?" I asked easily while I was trying to think of who had been reading my mind. Of course, Red could make a good guess, but I was damned sure Red wouldn't say anything.

"Don't pretend you don't know."

He kept at it, smiling. Maybe he noticed something in my face because he followed it up, laughing.

"Thelma! Weren't you and Thelma Parker sweethearts once?"

"Not exactly once."

Before he could answer, old Dag Petersen staggered in and made his lurching way to the bar. Holding on with both hands, he shook his head as if he had a bee in his tufted gray hair, then said, "Whiskey."

"I told you no an hour ago," Marvin said. "Go sleep it off, Dag."

"Blood." Dag said the word without even knowing it.

"They say Indians are the worst drunks in the world, but the damn Swedes go just as crazy as injuns, and they stay that way longer," Marvin said judiciously.

Dag smelled worse'n a wolf den, probably because he forgot to unbutton his pants before he peed, and I moved down the bar a ways toward Wade Filson.

Old Dag fumbled in his pocket, rocking back and forth, but couldn't find a coin. "Blood."

"Goddamn you!" Bud Mabry, next to Dag, blew up and hit the old man backhand across the face, driving him away from the bar. "Go somewhere else with your blood and leave me alone!"

Dag kept backing up until he backed into the corner, then he slid down to the floor and closed his eyes.

"Damned old fart, why don't he wash?" Mabry said, trying to cover his quick temper flash.

"He'll come out of it after a while," Marvin Bohn said.

So far as I could tell, except for Dag Petersen, no one knew about the blood on Turnbull's carpet that the Marshal and Mex Abrams had been whispering about.

I had it in mind to just ride old Buck up to the front door of the big house, walk on in, and take a look for myself.

But then what?

Then go out to the Tee-Bar and ask Beecher Turnbull where it come from?

That's what I wanted, all right, but blood was the Doc's profession and murder or mayhem was Marshal Witherspoon's. Mine was horses.

Yet I had the feeling in that room that most everyone in it had Jean Louise and the Turnbull brothers on their minds and that they could be moved from their normal routines to interfere in whatever was going on in the big house.

About this time, Dee Gibbon, with a look on his face like an alligator suckin' down a puppy, and Huerta came strolling in. If there'd been a whorehouse in town, I'd've sworn they'd just come from it, so slick and studdy and smug-like they looked.

Not nodding nor saying hello, they strutted to the bar, found a lot of space, and ordered a bottle of whiskey.

I could see right off I was going to get myself tangled in a hoolihan if I hung around those two very long, and I finished my beer, kind of sore that I didn't know any more than I ever did.

As I was turning away, in came Jake Levy, the little haberdasher, his bristly hair sticking out from the little round wool hat he always wore, his eyes spooked behind his spectacles, and his little mouth clamped shut so tight his full black beard met his mustache.

"Gimme a shot," he said quickly to Marvin Bohn, and then being about two feet shorter than me, looked up as if to see who it was.

He fitted the glass into the muff of his beard, jerked his head back, and set the empty glass down again.

"You hear about the blood?" he asked Marvin Bohn.

I watched Bohn. There was damned little in town he didn't know first, but his flat expression never changed, nor his expressionless voice. "No. What blood?"

"In the big house!" Jacob Levy burst out, as if the effort of holding in such a powerful piece of information had been boiling in his guts until it came out like hot steam from a safety valve. "Blood all over the place!"

The whole room waited for something to catch fire and burn the whole town down. No one breathed. Even Gibbon quit snickering at his private little joke.

"They ain't nobody there excepting Beecher and Metta Snapp," Wade Filson said slowly, like a brick mason laying a foundation with his level and plumb bob, making sure it was going to be founded properly. "And he's out at the ranch mostly," Filson added, looked at Levy.

"Blood? Who said?" Babe Silliman asked, keeping his cards close to his chest.

"Metta! Metta Snapp told Roberta Poffenberg, and she told my wife. She said there was blood on the carpet and in Dan's upstairs bedroom and in the kitchen, too!"

"Have you told Marshal Witherspoon?" I asked, wondering if Witherspoon and Abrams had been talking about the same thing.

"I just now did. I made it my duty to tell him first."

"What did he say?" Bolivar Cromwell boomed from a back table, where he was sitting with B. G. Hall, Buttonwillow's only preacher and mortician.

"He said he already knew about it and was looking into it." Jacob Levy's dome-shaped forehead was turning a dark red with righteous anger under his round hat, and I figured Witherspoon had told him to mind his own business.

Tuck Krendel, the barber, came in like a hungry bird dog looking for a choice partridge, his jug ears practically flapping in the breeze.

"Somebody say somethin' about trouble at the big house?"

"Metta Snapp's been talking."

"Talking blood!" Jacob Levy couldn't hold it in. He wasn't used to blood and broken bones and thorns and bullets, so it scalded his belly more than most.

Ed Lewis and Wayne Farnhorst came in, wanting to know what was going on.

Marvin Bohn kept busy filling glasses while it looked to me like every able-bodied man in town had congregated here except Witherspoon and Abrams.

"Foul play!" Fly Swinner croaked from the end of the bar, his broom propped in his armpit.

It was the one thing nobody'd been able to say, and it took a derelict to say it.

"Just a second," Doc said, putting his cards down, "there's all kinds of blood, and reasons for some to be shed in a house."

"But, Metta—"

"Better you all talk direct to Metta Snapp before you

start marching up the hill and stickin' your nose into a hornet's nest," Doc said.

"What do you know about it, Doc?" Wade Filson growled, turning to look down at the white-haired medico.

"It's not for me to say." Doc glared up at the big blacksmith. "Best you let Marshal Witherspoon do the job you're payin' him to do."

"He ain't doin' nothin' but connivin' with Mex Abrams," Jacob Levy burst out. "Nothing!"

"That's about what we're payin' him, too," Marvin Bohn rasped.

"If you all want me to investigate this matter and file the proper charges, I'm ready to go to work," Bolivar Cromwell boomed from the corner, then got up from his chair and came forward to the bar, looking at the men's faces questioningly.

No one looked back.

"Well?"

"How much?" Jacob Levy asked suspiciously.

"My usual fee. Depends on how long it takes to get it all straightened out."

"I don't think that'd work," Dad Crawford chuckled. "Lawyers don't live on straightening out things."

Nobody was even sure Bolivar Cromwell was a real lawyer anyway. Though they sometimes consulted him on legal papers, nobody had ever seen him in court, for all of his iron gray leonine locks and wide, puffy face that had started sagging early.

"I say we go up there, knock on the door, and tell Mr. Beecher Turnbull we aim to look at the evidence!" B. G. Hall bellowed, following Bolivar over from the table.

His interest had to be an embalming fee; for certain there was no one in the Prince Albert interested in a sermon. Sometimes folks called him Smiley behind his back because he never took that unearthly tragic and joyous half smile off his face, no matter what.

Somebody said they'd tipped his privy over on a

Halloween night and he came crawling out with that same holy happiness writ all over his torpid features, reaching from one big bushy sideburn to the other.

"I say we go up there politely, like charitable Christians, and ask what we can do to put these awful rumors to rest."

Bolivar Cromwell frowned and glared at B. G. Hall, but there wasn't anything he could say to stop the mortician, who, having smelt death like a coyote, would scratch around until he found a body.

In Turnbull's case, there would be money to pay for everything, from the embalming to using BG's lumber wagon he had painted black and called a hearse.

"You won't get anywhere pussyfootin' round," Wade Filson growled. "I say we go up there and tell Turnbull to open up."

"No, no," B.G. Hall held on, "we simply ask if there's some way we can help in this moment of tragedy, and view the remains."

"Supposin' there ain't any remains?" I put in, bothered by all the foolishness.

They shut up for a minute and looked at me suspiciously, as if I were in cahoots with Turnbull or Witherspoon.

"Besides, Beech is out at the ranch making the fall gather. He won't be back to town for a week," Dee Gibbon sang out, and laughed, "and I've got a notion Metta Snapp ain't goin' to let anyone in that house, if she values her job."

That stopped them. They could see that big bulldog of a woman meeting them at the front door.

"I could go up on a Christian mission," B.G. Hall suggested, but the men rapped their empty glasses on the bar and shook their heads, the wildness taken out of them by the image of Metta Snapp armed with a broom.

"They say he ain't been home in a week," Doc Meredith said, nailing the lid down.

"They say he's in the saddle at daybreak 'til past dark,

and he's keepin' all the hands on the run, too," Wayne Farnhorst added hesitantly. He'd known all along Beech wasn't home, but was afraid to speak up.

"Somebody said he was drunk," Ed Lewis said.

"He was last week," Tuck Krendel said. "It wasn't a pretty sight, I'll tell you."

"Sounds like a guilty conscience to me," Bolivar Cromwell added with a judicious nod.

"I reckon if my woman ran off with my kid brother, I wouldn't be goin' to any ice cream socials," Babe Silliman put in mildly.

"Whose side are you on anyways?" Wade Filson turned to stare at Babe.

Everyone knew Wade's wife had bought a sewing machine from Babe the time Wade went back to West Virginia to bury his daddy.

"I didn't know there was sides yet." Babe looked at him, his big spaniel eyes not blinking, his voice dead level.

What was likely to happen next would be Wade coming at Babe with his fist and Babe slipping out his hammerless Smith & Wesson .32-caliber five-shooter and equalizing the fight, but lucky for the blacksmith, somebody on a horse came thundering down the street like the devil was on his tail. In the next second of silence we heard the horse skid to a halt, and in a second Arnold Brennan's youngster came busting inside, his hat back down on his thin shoulders and held by a leather string, his long hair blown straight back.

"Where's Doc Meredith?" He came right out with it.

"That's me," Doc said, putting his cards down and moving his ante off to one side. "What's the hurry?"

"Man's been bushwhacked, but he's still alive."

"Where is he?"

"Out at our place. He just barely made it in a little bit ago."

Everyone's eyes were drawn like iron to a magnet over toward the runty Dee Gibbon and the skinny Mexican.

Doc murmured to the cardplayers, "I'll be back later," picked up his coins, got his bag from under the table, stood up, and said, "All right, son, think you can show me the road out to your place?"

"Just a moment, my boy," BG said, smiling angelically, "do we know the poor victim?"

"Pat Faulkner's his name," the boy replied as Doc steered him out the door.

=== 8 ===

P<small>AT</small> F<small>AULKNER WAS WELL KNOWN IN THE</small> J<small>UNIPER COUNTRY</small>
as a hardworking cattleman whose spread hadn't
amounted to much when he started, but who with his
wife and boys had weathered the bad times and used the
good times to improve his place, which neighbored to the
east of Brennan's and Bud Mabry's ranches.

Of course, he had every right to ride the open range,
and especially he had a right to be present at Beecher
Turnbull's fall gathering so he could collect whatever
strays were picked up.

"Goddamnit," Bud Mabry growled, "Pat was a friend
of mine."

"Mine, too," Frank Pedragal said. "I doubt he ever
said a mean word about anybody."

Everyone nodded at that, and Tuck Krendel said
softly, "Amen to that."

"By God, I'd sooner worry about some sonofabitch
shootin' riders in the back than Beech Turnbull's fence-
jumpin' heifer," Mabry said.

"Maybe it's all a part of the same horse," Ed Lewis said, a smart little smile on his thin lips.

"Hell, everybody else is right here," Wayne Farnhorst added.

"Not quite." B.G. Hall held up his hand in a rhetorical gesture. "Marshal Witherspoon and Mex Abrams are absent."

"But they're over at Ed's Cafe," Wade Filson put in.

"Red is over at Wolf Aufdemburg's," I said, so they wouldn't try accusing him.

"That's it, unless you count Ace Dietjen, and he's on his way south toward Ruby."

Dee Gibbon and Luis Huerta weren't even paying attention the way they were huddled up by themselves pretending no one else was around.

"Likely somebody could have done it and rode in before the kid," Wade Filson said heavily. "Likely they thought Pat was dead and wouldn't be found for a week."

He didn't say "he," he said "they." There wasn't much question about who he was talking about.

Now it would either lie there and fade away or somebody would pick it up and ride with it. Again the room became silent, like everyone had stopped breathing.

"You're saying it could be somebody right here and now." Mabry nodded. He wiped his face with his open hand, as if he could scrub some of the drink out of his head, and added, "Just who do you think that might be, Wade?"

"I'm not wearing a gun," Wade said simply. "You figure it out."

About then, the runt tossed a coin on the bar, and nodded to the Mexican. Huerta, looking neither left nor right, strolled toward the door, with Gibbon following behind, talking like there was someone listening.

"We got to get out to the ranch. Old Beech'll be mad enough to kick a hog barefoot if he figures we stopped by for a toddy the way he's been drivin' the boys lately. I'll sure be glad when we finish the roundup. I'm plumb sick of lookin' at the ass end of a cow all day . . ."

"Just a goddamned minute, Gibbon!" Bud Mabry yelled. He had turned and stepped clear of the bar and faced the runty little gunfighter directly.

Gibbon tried to act like he didn't hear, and Huerta slipped out the door.

"Goddamn you, you backshootin' sonofabitch!" Mabry roared this time so there was no mistaking his meaning.

Even as I was trying to get around Wade Filson and out of the line of fire, Mabry's hand dropped to the butt of his six-gun.

The runt was faster, because that was his trade. His hand snapped down in a blur and was cocking the .44 as he drew and fired.

He was fast, but hadn't too keen an eye. His first bullet went over Bud Mabry's shoulder and crazed the mirror behind the bar.

Marvin Bohn had dropped behind the bar, and most everyone else dived for cover, except big Wade Filson, who had me blocked.

Mabry fired and missed, and on top of his shot came Gibbon's second try, which puffed dust out of Bud's vest and turned him, but not before Bud had sent another slug off that smacked Gibbon in the upper shoulder, spinning him around and making his third shot go wild.

That wild shot ricocheted off the floor and came screaming. I felt a thump on my boot and then something like a big yucca thorn goin' into the calf of my leg, and the next thing I knew, my leg went out from under me and I was down on the floor.

Cussing some, I crawled around Wayne Farnhorst, keeping my eyes on Gibbon, who was now sitting up, holding on to his shoulder with his left hand.

Mabry's gun was loose on the floor and he was gritting

his teeth as he felt under his shirt with his gun hand and brought it out dripping with bright, fresh blood.

A second later the doors flapped open and Marshal Witherspoon stood there with his old hog leg in his right hand, and in his left the bunched-up collar of Huerta's shirt. Huerta himself looked dazed, hardly able to stand. He'd lost his hat, and I surmised Witherspoon had buffaloed him with that old Colt just outside the door.

"Get Doc," Gibbon whimpered, clutching at the broken shoulder.

"Doc's gone and you know it," Witherspoon said.

"Let me look," B.G. Hall said, and I felt better, because with his experience laying out gun-shot bodies, he probably knew more about bullet wounds than Doc did.

"Give me some towels," he said, and Marvin Bohn came up from behind the bar with some flour sacks and a short twelve-gauge greener.

B.G. Hall pulled off Gibbon's vest and ripped the shirt loose, exposing a welter of blood leaking out of the shoulder. Folding up one of the towels, he put it over the wound and told Gibbon to hold it on tight.

"Either Bud's short-loading his cartridges, or that bullhide vest is tougher than most," he observed, like he was a professor talking to a class of medical students. "The bullet entered the upper clavicle, broke through the shoulder, but had not sufficient velocity to exit. Doc will remove it when he returns."

"Save the palaver, Smiley," Mabry rasped out, so that everyone turned to see his face turning pale as he sat on the dirty floor, leaning back against the bar.

BG wiped his bloody hands on one of the flour sacks and strolled over, put a sack on the floor for his knees to kneel on, unbuttoned Bud's shirt, loosened his belt and the top button of his jeans, and pulled the shirt away from the wound.

Bud's side was bleeding a lot and the skin was turning

purple. BG took another flour sack and, holding Bud's hand away, wiped the blood off his side.

"God be praised," BG smiled, "the Almighty is looking after you, Bud. More towels, please," he said, looking up at Marvin Bohn before going back to cleaning off the wide band of blood.

"Merely a scrape across the second rib. God gave you a strong rib, Mr. Mabry. I trust you'll come to church soon to render your appreciation."

"Just fix it—" Bud said with his teeth gritted, ready to faint.

BG made up a long, thick compress, laid it on the gouge, then asked Wade Filson for his belt.

"A perfect fit, Wade," BG said cheerfully, and cinched the belt around the compress tight enough to make Bud faint away, but also to stop most of the bleeding.

"Anybody else?" He looked around contented as a buzzard roostin' on top a slaughterhouse.

"I got a little nick when you've got time," I said, not really wanting to have him look, but not knowing anything else to do. He moved his knee pad over next to me, looked at my face first, then asked, "Where is it?"

"My leg," I said, wondering why he couldn't see it.

He looked down and saw some blood that was starting to leak over the top of my boot.

"Yes, indeedy," he muttered, and tried to ease the boot off, but I guess my face flinched, so he took out his big jackknife and sliced down the side of my damned near brand-new Carson boot, so it would fall off, then ruined my pants leg by slicing up the rolled-up cuff, so he could see the hole in my calf just below the knee.

"Lord be praised," he declared happily. "The bone is not broken and God Almighty has spared your knee."

After he'd cleaned it up, I could see how the wild shot had torn through the meat and out the other side, taking some rags and threads along with it.

He asked Marvin for a bottle of forty rod, tipped it

down the hole, and squeezed the muscle, which made me cuss.

In a second, though, he tied another flour sack around my knee and got to his feet.

"Praise be to heaven above, the good Lord has spared these men. Let's have a drink!"

"You tired?" I heard a voice say, and I looked up to see that familiar flat little face inside a big head, the hard, dark eyes boring into mine.

9

MA LEWIS PUT ME IN THE DOWNSTAIRS ROOM THAT FACED the street because she didn't want to be climbing stairs looking after me, even after I told her and BG and Red about forty times I could walk as good as a rooster in deep mud.

"Don't make a nevermind," BG insisted. "You got a regular rat's nest inside the muscle, and if you don't want to be peggin' around like old Ed the rest of your life, you'll pay attention to me."

"Do what he says," Red said. "I'll look after the ranch."

Nothing would do but I had to soak the leg in water, Epsom salts, whiskey, and carbolic acid, which Ma Lewis kept hot by dipping in water off the stove until the copper boiler was ready to run over; then she'd dip it out again and put more hot in it.

Meantime I was supposed to knead the calf muscle all it could stand so as to float out the contaminations.

BG was right about that. Little tangles of thread, flakes

of leather, sawdust, splinters, hair, weed stems, and likely horse manure drifted out into the hot water toward dark time, along with an ooze of blood serum.

"It's workin'," Ma said, lugging in another bucket of hot water, "but if it was me, I'd jam a chaw of tobacco in there and bind her tight. That's the way I was taught."

"Reckon BG wants the stuff out instead of in," I said, trying to be polite to the gaunty, hulking, tobacco-chewing woman.

"But it's still bleedin'."

"It's part of the cleanin' maybe." I didn't want to argue. For damned sure I wasn't going to let her stick her quid into that aching hole in my leg.

"It's agin nature and can't be did," she said, looking up at heaven.

"I'll be walkin' on it tomorrow, ma'am."

"Set still. I don't mean to run you off with my jay-bird jabberin'. It's just I ain't never got no one to talk to."

"Ed's always around."

"Even if he was, he ain't never got nothin' to say. Always on the prowl like a damn old tomcat, but to hear him tell it, he's splittin' kindlin' for me day and night."

"Ed said he heard a ruckus over at the big house the other evening . . ." I said, fishing for her side of it.

"Likely he did hear something, but I wouldn't set much store by it."

I couldn't very well ask her if her husband was a liar and a night prowler, and maybe even a Peeping Tom, much as I wanted to. She would know if anyone did, but of course she wouldn't ever say, or he'd take a club to her.

"You reckon they were fightin' serious enough to draw blood?"

"You never know about folks in big houses," she said,

nodding mysteriously. "They got their ways, and that Jean Louise, underneath all her cavortin' around like a fat pony in wild oats, never belonged up there."

"How do you mean?" I asked, trying to not look like I was nosy.

"Nosy, ain't you?" she came back at me with a snort. "I mean underneath that big, bright smile and bug eyes was somethin' else. Poor folks have poor ways."

With that she picked up the bucket of cold water and went on back to the kitchen, leaving me to squeeze the trash out of my leg.

Doc Meredith made it back to town after dark. After he'd had a couple of drinks at the Prince Albert he came over to the rooming house to look at my damage.

"Pat?" I asked him, as he peered down at my leaking leg.

"Hard dyin'," he said. "Nothin' I could give him to heal up the mess his liver was in, so I gave him all the whiskey he could hold down and saw him off."

"Back-shot?"

"Long range. Whoever did it might not have even known who it was. Mind you, I'm not telling this over at the P.A.; they'd be hanging Dee Gibbon and Huerta right this minute if they knew how devilish it was."

"You think it was them two?"

"You saw 'em in the bar, how they was grinning like baked possums."

"But it coulda been somebody else," I argued mildly to keep him talking.

"Who? Turnbull? No, he pays his men to peel his broncs."

"Maybe somebody else that wants to lay the blame on Tee-Bar."

"I think I know every polecat in Juniper country." Doc shook his head. "But I'll want a jury to convict those two before I go to their hanging."

"You think the boys will wait?"

"Witherspoon's sent off for a state ranger."

"That'll take days."

"Witherspoon ain't a man to fool with," Doc said, getting tiredly to his feet. "Now you get a night's sleep and don't plan on working until that yellow color around the wound goes away. If it gets any worse, I'm going to have to sharpen my bone saw."

He wrapped my leg so I could sleep and went on his way while I lay back on the bed trying to close my eyes and forget everything that had happened, but there was always that one vision of Jean Louise smiling, her eyes twinkling mischievously, her face open and un-afraid, her fine light brown hair childlike in its simple ponytail.

Was she dead? Would Beecher kill her and his own brother out of jealousy and pride?

It didn't ring right. Beecher Turnbull was a boss, a man who fancied himself as a general telling the troops to go do the dirty work. That's why his ranch hands were so sullen most of the time, why Gibbon and Huerta always had money in their pockets.

I sure appreciate knowin' you, Wesley.

Then I fell into a sleep of complete weariness and I dreamed of Jeanie with the light brown hair.

Morning was better, because the tiredness was gone, even if the hole in my leg didn't look any better and was sore as a boil on a bear's nose.

Doc came over and changed the wrapping, and old Ed Lauder pegged in, carrying a spare crutch.

"I don't use this anymore," he said, "not once I learned to trust my peg. You're welcome to borrow it for a couple days if you want to get down to the Prince Albert."

"I just don't think I can ride a crutch, Ed," I said. "But thank you anyway."

"Give it a try and surprise yourself." He laughed and went on back to his cafe.

I got myself out of bed and crutched around the room some and learned to keep my leg bent so it wasn't bumping on anything.

Ma Lewis's breakfast was some more simple than Red's, being boiled mush with nothing added to it, not a raisin or a currant or cinnamon or milk or sugar or salt. Simple mush plain.

Afterward I aimed down the boardwalk to Aufdemburg's Mercantile and put up with his talk about how the town was going downhill, and how they figured to hang the two backshooters today or tonight, as soon as they could all get together and agree on it.

"I told them I'd furnish the ropes, ya!" he snorted like an old mossback bull pawin' the ground. It was a good show, except I knew that's all he'd furnish. He'd be hiding down in the basement, taking inventory, when it came time for action.

His boots were about half the quality for twice the price, but I couldn't put the one on my left foot just yet.

"Look here, Mr. Bengard," Aufdemburg said, after he'd sold me the boots, "gaiters is what you need for a while. You can't bang your foot if you got the gaiters on."

They were loose and soft slip-ons with a high tongue you could grab on to, and while I was sitting there, he eased one around my sore foot so nice and easy like, I bought a pair of them, too. With a boot on my right foot and a soft, floppy gaiter on my left, I looked kind of loco, but I felt better with my foot being covered up.

Pegging back up to the rooming house, I left off my parcel and crossed over to Marshal Witherspoon's office in front of the jail.

He was sitting in a wired-together oak chair outside the office door, whittling curls off a piece of soft pine, looking harmless enough, except for the pair of Peacemakers riding down from his gun belt, a two-bore, sawed-off twelve-gauge leaning against the wall on his right, and a Marlin repeater rifle leaning against the door frame on his left.

"You ever check on the blood in the big house?" I asked him after we went through the polite preliminaries.

"Not yet. Can't very well leave my prisoners."

"Why don't you deputize somebody?" I asked.

"Mex Abrams is naggin' me. Bud Mabry is chawin' my backside. Jake Levy is moanin' at me. Wade Filson wants action. Now what's your interest?" Witherspoon drawled, keeping his curl peeling off the knife blade.

"I guess I ain't got any interest, except I'm plumb tired of lookin' over my shoulder every time I go outside to take a leak," I said, seeing Doc approaching.

"Ain't nobody in town I'd trust to guard my prisoners," he said, "at least until the sheriff from Ponca Sink or a state ranger comes to take 'em away."

"Why don't you deputize your wife, Witherspoon?" Doc suggested, bright as a sparrow. "There ain't a man in town would go against her."

"Possible." Witherspoon nodded, folded up his jackknife, and dusted the shavings off his lap. Then he rose, went to the door, and yelled, "Emily!"

There were a couple of rooms next to the jail that could be reached from a side door of the office, and in a minute, Emily Witherspoon, a sawed-off, plump little lady with a face like a prairie dog, came out carrying a broom, as if she'd just been interrupted in a life-and-death operation.

"What is it?"

"You set here with the two-bore across your lap and shoot the first man that looks cross-eyed at you."

"I've got my chores to do," she protested.

"Do what I damn say," Wolford barked.

She set her broom aside, sat down in the chair, and carefully drew the shotgun up on her bountiful lap.

"Who else goes?" He looked at Doc.

"Bolivar Cromwell maybe."

"All right. The windbag, the banker, and Jake Levy. Bud don't feel like getting out of bed this morning," Witherspoon said.

"I'll bring my buggy around," Doc said, walking through the alleyway that would take him down to Dad Crawford's livery.

When Doc returned with the buggy, I managed to climb up to the horsehide seat, and after a minute Witherspoon and Cromwell showed up in Jake Levy's jump-seater and led the way through town up the slope toward the big white house.

"They say Turnbull is staying out at the ranch," I said.

"We want to see all this blood everybody's got on their minds," Doc said.

"I hope it ain't there," I said quietly.

"You got bit by that pretty little bug?" Doc glanced over at me sympathetically.

"Some, I guess. I hardly knew her, though, except to speak her name when we met."

"I suppose for a loner like you, that's a bunch," Doc said with a nod.

"Ain't nothin' I can do about it if I was a mind to." I was plenty glad I had Doc to talk to.

"Keep thinking that way and you'll be all right."

We followed Jake's rig into the circular driveway. The men climbed down to the ground and fooled around, hoping, I suppose, that someone would come out and save them the trouble of climbing the steps and knocking at the door.

"I guess we come up here for something," Witherspoon growled, and led the way. Using the handrail, I made it up easy enough, and by then Witherspoon had used the brass door-knocker, which was the only one in town and probably in all of Lander County.

The wide oak door opened, but effectively blocking it

was the broad bulk of Metta Snapp. She wore a gray shapeless dress and a towel wrapped around her head, and in one massive hand she held a turkey feather duster.

She glanced around at all of us, then put her flinty eyes on Witherspoon.

"What is it?"

"We come to find out about the blood—"

"What blood?" she rasped.

"The blood we hear is all over the floors and walls," Bolivar Cromwell took over. He was at least as big as her and used to booming his voice at double strength.

"Why?" She wasn't a bit fazed and everyone was ready to turn around and scat, but Jacob Levy hung on.

"Because there's reports of a terrible fight that may have resulted in murder."

"Hogwash." She started to close the door.

"Just a minute, Metta," came the voice of Beecher Turnbull. "Let the gentlemen in."

She opened the door and stepped inside, revealing Turnbull coming forward. He was in his shirtsleeves and his heavy face seemed to have melted down like tallow since I'd last seen him. He hadn't shaved for a few days, which added to his wasted look, and beneath his sunken eyes were pouchy bars of gray.

In his hand he held a glass that was half full of an amber liquid that smelled like brandy.

"Come in, gentlemen," he said, putting up a smile. "Welcome to my humble home."

We all took our hats off and moved inside.

The walls were painted white and had pictures and needlework mottoes hanging on them, and there was more than plenty of heavy walnut furniture.

"Care for a drink, gentlemen?" Beecher offered, but made no move toward the sideboard, where several odd-shaped bottles were mixed up with cut-glass goblets.

"It's not every day I'm so honored . . ."

"We don't mean to pry . . ." Witherspoon muttered.

117

"Not at all. Come in and see for yourself what a fine housekeeper Mrs. Snapp is. You'll observe the place is spotless."

He led us past the parlor into a kind of study where there was a desk and books and a couple of easy chairs.

"Unfortunately, my wife is away . . ."

"That's what we came to see about," Bolivar Cromwell said.

"And you, Mr. Abrams, are you, too, concerned about my wife's well-being?"

"Better to clear up the rumors," Mex Abrams said, his voice, as always, cold as a Scotch maiden's crotch.

Being the last of the group, I didn't have to listen to them talk, and could put my attention on the floors and walls.

There'd been nothing out of order in the parlor, but in the study something was wrong, and then I noticed it was that the lace curtains were gone from the big window that looked on east toward the Tee-Bar ranch.

The rug, too, looked strange, because it was a lighter color than the big one next to it. I looked around and saw that big Metta Snapp had stayed back in the parlor. Leaning against a walnut chair and using my right foot to hold down the gaiter, I slipped my bare foot out and touched it into the carpet. If it wasn't wet, it sure as hell was damp.

I slipped the gaiter on again and listened.

"She's taken my younger brother to a Sacramento doctor . . . begging your forgiveness, Dr. Meredith, I'm sure she meant no disrespect—"

His eyes back in their caves were red, and he was holding himself together by assuming a jaunty role that was as false as a billy goat with feathers.

"When do you expect them back?"

"It all depends upon what the doctor says. Anything else—a cigar, perhaps . . . ? Would you care to stay for lunch? I'll tell Mrs. Snapp to set more places."

He seemed to me like a bronc fightin' a lot of ropes, including one around his neck.

"I've just finished the fall gather . . . the calf crop is better than expected . . ."

"How did they travel?" Jacob Levy got it out and slipped it in between the disjointed phrases of the embattled man.

"Who? Oh, my dear wife and brother—they thought the trail too rough for the buggy . . . so, we all rode to Fallon, where they took the stage to Ponca Sink. I presume they took the train from there—"

"You brought back their horses then."

"Not much else I could do, seeing as how far away we are . . . it's difficult for a young lady to live here . . . the town needs more money, more social affairs, more people . . ."

"Problem is the people are being bushwhacked faster than they're coming in," Marshal Witherspoon said. "I've got Gibbon and Huerta in jail."

"Drunk?"

"No, they started acting mighty strange last night when we got word about Pat Faulkner."

"Pat Faulkner? I'm sorry to hear . . . fine man . . . a little behind the times . . . bit off more than he could chew with that ranch . . . I'll have to call upon the family—"

"I wouldn't, if I were you," Mexican Abrams said. "They may figure you're responsible."

"There are others besides myself looking for bargains . . ."

His big head swayed on his humped shoulders and his voice was becoming monotonously sweet and cheery.

"So you claim your wife and brother are alive in Sacramento?" Bolivar Cromwell boomed out accusingly.

"Claim? My dear sir, it is not a claim, it is a fact."

"That can't be proven." Cromwell kept at him, trying to push him over the edge.

119

"If you doubt my word, then please go over to Sacramento and speak to Dr. Benton Hartford. Is there anything . . . else . . . ? I'm late for—"

"What do you want to do about Gibbon?"

"Some ranchers hire men to ride bucking broncs for five dollars a head, and some hire men to kill other men at so much a head, but I do neither. Gibbon and Huerta were hired to keep my cowhands honest and the general public from rustling my property. I paid them off when Mr. Bengard reported an attack on him. I do not condone murder. Is that what you wanted to hear, gentlemen? Let me say it again . . . I do not condone murder—"

"I'll have a hard time keeping them if the ranchers decide to come in before the trial," Witherspoon said.

He was right. The town was too small and docile to do anything violent on its own, but if the outside ranchers, hombres like me and Red, the Faulkners and Mabrys, took a notion to swing Gibbon and Huerta, they'd damned well do it.

"Hang them!" Turnbull boomed. "If they're guilty, let them pay with their lives! No more buttermilk justice. Any person that murders another must be punished!"

He was fired up and saying what he felt for a change, but it made my backbone shiver when I wondered if Jean Louise and Dan had wronged the big he-boar. What punishment would he lay on them?

I looked out the window, ashamed to witness the half-hidden anguish and rage in the man. I'd rather fight him any day than peek into his secret sorrows, which, whether he'd brought them on himself or not, were still too personal for me to look at.

Instead, I looked out over the long, flat, arid land toward his ranch headquarters. Then I was looking at the rising heat waves, bunches of cattle and loose bands of horses, then nearer was the wagon road cutting across, and closer was the big corral behind the house, and a clothesline where the lace curtains were moving in the breeze, then I could see a straggly, dusty rose garden doing poorly. Next to it, near the wash shed, a mound of trash smoldered in a ring of rocks. It could have been anything—damp leaves, rags, scraps of leather, old clothes—but the piece of bright red ribbon lying outside the fire ring caught my eye.

I shut my eyes and felt my stomach roll over as I saw the face of the honest-eyed tomboy with her whiskey-colored hair tied up with a red silk ribbon.

I sure appreciate knowin' you, Wesley . . .

It was still there when I looked again, and I touched Witherspoon's arm with my elbow.

He turned, read my face, and followed my eyes.

His long, hound-dog face paled and it occurred to me that he might have had a way of caring for Jean Louise like everybody else in town.

He set his bony shoulders and faced Beecher Turnbull.

"Would you mind if we looked around outside?"

"Whatever for?" Turnbull's eyes narrowed, and he found some of his old arrogance to lean on. "Don't you have anything better to do than poke through people's rubbish?"

Witherspoon didn't wait. We followed him down the hall, through the kitchen, where the powerful Metta Snapp glared at us, then down the steps into the backyard.

Witherspoon picked up a pitchfork on the way and quickly dragged the smoldering pile of clothing outside the fire pit and dippered some water from the washhouse to put out the smoking embers.

Even though most of it was burnt, we could see that there was an expensive dress, some unmentionables, stockings, high-buttoned patent leather shoes, and the red silk ribbon.

We could also make out a small man's worsted suit, a dress shirt, shoes, socks, and a pair of new kid gloves, along with sheets from a half-charred pad of paper.

I recognized the dress as the one Jean Louise had worn the day I met her and Dan in Aufdemburg's Mercantile.

Witherspoon picked up the remnant of the stationery pad, looked it over, and handed it to me.

"I can't make heads nor tails from it," he growled. "What do you think?"

I read the few lines remaining.

> Now the nightly desert of my vacant mind
> Floods with wild amber tresses,
> And life leaps up . . .

I knew it was Dan's poem, because it was some of what I'd always wanted to say but couldn't.

"Beats me," I said, handing the page back to Witherspoon.

— 10 —

By God, Turnbull, I want an explanation for this!"
Witherspoon said loudly, and I saw the little smile of
triumph form on Mex Abrams's twisted lips.

In one jump he could gobble up Turnbull's share of
Juniper Valley, which, added to his own holdings in
town, would make him boss. Turnbull had done all the
dirty work, and the prize was ready for the taking.

"You can see it's old clothes being burnt." Turnbull
wasn't backing up.

"They're pretty new for burning in this country," Doc
said with a strange sadness in his voice. I reckoned he
was another one of us who was fond of Jean Louise but
too knotheaded to do anything about it. "The gloves
have never been worn."

"This is my own private, personal business. If I want to
burn up the whole damn place, it's nothing to you,"
Turnbull came back, strong and arrogant again.

"But they're not your clothes, they're Jeanie's and
Dan's," Bolivar Cromwell declared. "Why would you
burn their goods?"

"Because they won't need them anymore," Turnbull replied softly, looking at the ground.

"If they're dead, you're going to need legal representation. I'll be glad to help all I can . . ."

I could see that another vulture besides Abrams was ready to pick the bones of the range hog.

"If he's murdered that girl, he won't need a lawyer," Abrams growled.

"Just tell me the truth," Witherspoon said. "Why?"

"It can be lonely alone in the big house," Turnbull explained reasonably. "If there's nothing else to do . . . I clean out the closets. It's good for the nerves."

I didn't believe it, no matter how shaky he looked. Neither did anyone else. He wasn't that crazy.

"They're both dead," Mex Abrams said sourly. "He killed 'em and buried them out in some godforsaken hole. Arrest him!"

"I need to see some bodies first," Marshal Witherspoon growled, putting his hound-dog eyes on Turnbull. "Where are they?"

Turnbull shook his head slowly, the muscles in his jaws swelling as he tried to gather up strength enough to carry on.

"They're in Sacramento," Turnbull said softly, as if he was saying something he didn't want to.

"You want to confess right now and get it over with?" Witherspoon persisted, while trying to sound kindly and sympathetic.

As Turnbull shook his head, Jacob Levy piped up, "He said they were in Sacramento. You can't do a thing until you prove otherwise."

"I'm not holding court out here." Witherspoon faced us, then turned back to Turnbull and said, "Tell the truth and shame the devil."

Turnbull had found his strength by then and said, "How many times does it take to get a simple message across to you?"

"You want it the hard way, I'll look for more evidence." Witherspoon was trying to bluff, but he'd played his high cards already.

"Christ! How much evidence do you need?" Mex Abrams snarled like a cat that has been cheated of its mouse. "Look at him!"

"You ever married?" Witherspoon came back at the banker, tired of his hurry-up.

"I'm not crazy—" the banker began to say, faking a smile and trying to cover up with a joke.

"Then you don't know how it feels to lose someone you trust," Witherspoon interrupted, and I saw something extra in him that I'd missed before. He had a front like a stone wall, but along the way he'd had some disappointments and held them back in his head maybe to use in times like this.

In a way, I had that same feeling, only mine was based on woolgathering dreams where I felt better thinking that my dream girl was decent and treated me fair. Now I didn't know. If she'd run off, then it was like she'd run away from me. The hurt I felt would be magnified a thousand times if I was her husband.

Maybe she'd flashed that wide smile at Marshal Witherspoon, too, and maybe he'd had his dreams same as me, and maybe he felt the same way.

"I don't want you leavin', understand me?" Witherspoon said to the big rancher. "You stay right here."

"I have no reason to leave," Beecher Turnbull said. "Where would I go?"

Witherspoon turned away decisively and we walked around the house to the front driveway. I was last, going slow on the crutch, and by the time I got to Doc's buggy, I'd had enough of crutchin'. I figured I'd either set or ride, one or the other, from here on out.

"Leg bothering?" Doc asked as he shook the reins and got the fat gray mare to moving.

"No more'n if a red-hot fishhook was in it."

"That's a healthy sign." He smiled. "When it starts dulling down to a swollen ache and begins to stink, then we'll start to worry."

"Let me off at the P.A.," I said. "I'm gettin' plumb barn-sour."

"You can bet it'll liven up some."

"You're talkin' about Gibbon?"

"Mabry will have his clan riding to every little rancher in the Juniper, spreading the news, and forming up a committee."

"Likely that Gibbon sonofabitch burned my neck. I'm not feelin' sorry for him."

"But it's the same as Turnbull. There's no evidence against any of them."

"They settled their hash yesterday, by the way they acted. If Pat Faulkner hadn't made it home, nobody would've known for a while he'd been bushwhacked, and it'd be too oozy by then to lay it on anybody, but this is fresh as a smokin' cow pie."

"Don't remind me," Doc said. "I saw him die, and I have a hard time respecting the human race at those times."

I pegged into the dark saloon and had nothing to say when Marvin Bohn put a glass of beer in front of me and asked, "Been busy?"

Let the damn gossipers gossip. I was fed up to my hat with it. I'd been thinking that spending a month at a time out on the range with no company except Red might be hard on a man's sociability, but I was beginning to appreciate the company of that dumb Indian more'n these town buzzards.

Fly Swinner was pushing the sawdust around, and I noticed he'd mopped at the blood from the night before and maybe got the thickest part of it, then scattered fresh sawdust over the worst of it.

If I had any sense I'd climb up on old Buck and make a beeline for the ranch.

It wasn't my leg holding me back, though, it was I

wanted to see whether Mabry could raise up a crew of hangmen.

It'd have to happen this afternoon, because the state ranger would be in by tomorrow and take Huerta and Gibbon off for a trial—if it ever came to that—in Carson.

So, I figured to have a front seat for the show. I'd earned it when Gibbon's ricochet punched my leg, and I had some personal interest in seeing him hang whether he was guilty or not.

Seeing I was a little salty, Marvin Bohn went on down to the end of the bar to talk with John Evans, an old tommy-knocker of a prospector who always carried a few rocks in his pocket to show around.

He'd say things like "good values," "eroded colors," "rich dirt," or some such mineral talk, but he'd been pounding on rocks all his life and never found enough pay dirt to keep him alive. Generally he lived off stakes folks gave him in case he really did hit a bonanza. I'd paid my small dues like everybody else, makin' sure he had enough to eat and could do what he liked best.

Ace Dietjen strolled in after I had taken a chair where I could stretch out my leg.

"How's the horse business?" I asked, not much caring.

"Why don't you sell me a few and make us both rich," he said, not caring either.

"I doubt if we'll gather any more until spring."

"It's a good time right now," he murmured.

"You sayin' the bushwhackin' is over with?"

"I'd say now is the time to see how many tricks Mexican Abrams has up his sleeve. He's the new dealer."

"Not if Turnbull can pull his guts together," I said for the sake of argument.

"Losin' his wife might make him meaner'n a bagful of rattlesnakes," Ace said. "Traded a preacher a horse once . . . had to put corks up my horse's nose because he kept makin' such a horrible death rattle when he breathed. Preacher was nice as pie and gave me an old ringboned mule and five dollars to boot. Just before I left, I pulled the strings and got my corks back without him seein' me. Next mornin' that nice, gentle pastor come runnin' down to my room carryin' a ten-bore goosegun screechin' how he was cheated.''

"Then?"

"I told him I'd trade him back his mule, but of course I kept the five dollars boot money for my trouble." Ace smiled slightly, remembering. "Folks change when things don't work out the way they expect."

About then a couple riders, strangers to me, came in and walked straight to the bar. Lean and carved sharp by the hard country, they were dressed like working cowpunchers and ordered straight whiskey.

"No offense, but are you boys looking for work?" Marvin Bohn asked, setting out the bottle.

"We ranch over by Ruby," the taller one said, shaking his head. "Pat Faulkner was kin."

Plainly they hadn't rode all the way over to the Juniper to shake hands with Gibbon.

"Word travels fast," Marvin Bohn said, his flat face never changing.

"One of the Mabry boys sent word," the short one said. "We was afraid you folks'd hang 'em before we got here."

Not long after, more Faulkner kin drifted in. They was more the bib-overall types, worrying some about associating with the regular rawhide cowboys, and they weren't carrying any guns you could see. They kept to a table toward the corner and drank some beer.

"The gatherin' of the jury," Ace observed. "Mabry's choice."

Soon enough three other riders showed up. Their name was Westfall, and they were trying to raise cattle on north of the Lazy B and not having much success at it. As far as I knew, there hadn't been any Westfalls bushwhacked, but of course, it had been on their minds enough to bring them into Buttonwillow.

128

Buttonwillow had never had a hanging, nor even a boot hill.

Then come in a couple cowboys name of Harlan that didn't mean anything to me, but Ace remembered it was a Harlan had been bushwhacked a couple, three years before.

Everybody had taken it for granted that those dead riders were loners, but it turned out some of 'em had families that never wanted to claim them before.

"Because they knew they were rustlin' and didn't want to own up to it," I said, seeing how it was going.

"I never saw the P.A. so crowded this early in the day," Ace drawled, looking around. "Hangings are surely a popular event. Beats Sunday vespers all to flinderjigs."

Faulkner's brothers came in after a while, and the noise was on the rise. Those Faulkners were Southern mountain boys, and what they didn't know about cows, they made up in hard work.

"I hear they never learned to ride back in Carolina," Ace said. "They'd rather run a bull down barefoot."

"I never knew a bull to run from a man afoot."

"I'm just sayin' what I heard," Ace said. "Look at them."

They were big, tall, rangy rannies, same as Pat Faulkner'd been.

"Pat was ridin' when he was shot," I said to keep it straight.

"Pat was the first one out here, and he was taggin' along with Bud Mabry, so he had to ride."

I couldn't see that it was going to make any difference for Dee Gibbon or Luis Huerta. For damned sure there was plenty enough straight up and down men in the P.A. to do a hanging.

Ace allowed he was hungry enough to eat cat, and I reckoned we'd better fill up before the town was cleaned out of vittles.

We stood outside the P.A. a minute, seeing how the street had filled up with horses and youngsters trotting their ponies up and down, showing off, while the women-folk in their town dresses paraded around, looking in the few windows and crowding in and out of Aufdemburg's Mercantile.

"I swear, if we had a hangin' every Saturday, the railroad would run a spur over from Carson," Ace said.

"Where would they get the men to hang?" I asked.

"Maybe the local businessmen would volunteer some of their family, or maybe they could hire some Mexicans cheap."

I had to laugh at Ace's mordant humor.

"Of course," I said, as we crossed the street between wagons, "somebody's goin' to have to explain it all to Marshal Witherspoon and his bride."

"I'd guess by the time they're ready for the hemp dance, Witherspoon will be out lookin' for next week's show."

Ed's was crowded but there were a couple extra seats at Bolivar Cromwell's table and he motioned for us to join him.

"I see you're fixin' up for the festival," he said as we sat down.

"Can't you find some need of a lawyer in all this?" I asked, curious as to what he was thinking.

"Unfortunately"—he jabbed the air with his fork—"the accused have neither money, property, nor friends. Who am I to stand in the way of justice?"

"They were workin' for Beecher Turnbull," Ace said softly.

"It may be they were in his employ," the leonine-headed lawyer declared, "but it is not certain that he gave them orders to murder any stray rider who happened to trespass on his range."

"I keep sayin' it's public range," I said. "But Turnbull has lied about it so much people believe him."

"Indeed, that's true," Cromwell nodded, "but the basic point is did he order Gibbon and Huerta to shoot those men."

"For sure they'll claim he did," Ace put in.

"I understand they are not talking," Cromwell said. "They don't realize what's happening out here."

"They must think they'll be exonerated for lack of evidence and then come back to Turnbull for some big hush money," Ace said thoughtfully.

"Indeed, Mr. Turnbull is flirting with disaster on every front," Cromwell nodded with pleasure. "I only hope he'll let me save him."

We ordered the blue plate special, which was Swiss steak with gravy, mashed potatoes, baked navy beans, and custard for dessert.

As Cromwell rose in all his majesty to leave, I said, "Right or wrong, somebody ought to defend that pair of backshooters."

"I will nominate Reverend B. G. Hall for such a spiritually rewarding task," Bolivar Cromwell declared grandly.

I had to laugh. The whole of Buttonwillow had gone loco.

We were starting to scrub the red gravy off our plates with Melba's homemade white bread when Marshal Witherspoon came in the door, saw us, and moved through the crowd to our table.

"Howdy, boys," he said heavily, taking a seat.

"Who's watchin' the prisoners?" Ace asked quietly.

"I've deputized B. G. Hall and Jake Levy. They're the best I could find so far."

"Don't say no more," I said, looking him right in the eye. "I ain't on one side or the other."

"I lean toward quick justice," Ace said.

"I need help." Witherspoon would have begged maybe, but deep down he only wanted to do his job, not cause any harm on account of a pair of bushwhackers.

"You forget he just missed takin' out my neck bone," I said. "I ain't pullin' on any rope, but I don't want 'em loose to do it all over again."

"I reckon that's what the folks are afraid of," Ace

nodded. "That pair gets over to Carson, there won't be any witnesses against them."

"I'll be there," Witherspoon said. "I'll testify."

"You couldn't testify to much more than a shootin' in the Prince Albert," I said. "There was never a witness to those bushwhackings."

"So how can you hang 'em?" Witherspoon asked like it was my fault.

"I'm not. I'm not buying drinks for the house. I'm not donating the twine. I'm not makin' any speeches, and I'm sure not standin' up alongside B. G. Hall and Jake Levy."

"Well"—he touched his gray walrus mustache mournfully and got to his feet—"I tried my best."

"And your conscience is clear," Ace said so he could take it any way he wanted.

After the custard, we stood out on the boardwalk a while, watching the movement of horses, vehicles, and people back and forth. Hell, the town was only two blocks long and one wide, and you couldn't hardly find a corner to pee in there was so much activity. After Ace had smoked half a cigar we made our way back inside the Prince Albert.

My leg was feeling stronger, if not any better. The knitting of torn muscles is never joyful, and the hole through my leg was substantial.

Babe Silliman joined us in the back of the P.A., and I saw that Fly Swinner was trying to wait on the tables, but he was so drunk he couldn't carry a tray.

Bud Mabry had been brought in by his sons, and was sitting in a chair close to the bar, where the forty rod was flowing.

"When?" I asked Babe Silliman.

"Sure before sunset."

"When the alcohol level is equal to the sum of the aggravation and the joy," Ace Dietjen said like a professor.

"What do you think of Jean Louise and Dan runnin' off?" I asked.

"I am disappointed some in that girl," Babe said. I thought his expression carried some of that loss that others had shown and that was riding in my own heart.

"How many broken hearts do you suppose she left behind?" Ace asked, as if it was an idle question.

"I'd say it's more like broken dreams," Babe said quietly, dead serious. "It's too bad."

I kept out of it, figuring my dream was my own to keep however I wanted to keep it.

I dream of Jeanie with the light brown hair . . .

Little boys were running in now, tugging on their dads' shirttails, bringing messages from their mommas, mainly meaning, "What are you waiting for—it's getting late and it's a long ways home."

The men, though, were enjoying the camaraderie and the liquor, and didn't want to be hurried.

Finally one of them, a Mabry it looked like, got tired of his boy nagging him, and said, "All right, goddamnit, tell her we'll take care of it right away!"

The little boy ran out with the commitment, which in effect was a promise, because everybody had heard it and the alcohol level was just about equal to the sum of the aggravation and expectant joy.

"Let's finish the bottle and go get 'em," Bud Mabry said, holding up his glass for someone to fill.

The room quieted down and the men put on serious looks and called for no more drinks, so that in a few minutes, Marvin Bohn was busy collecting bottles and glasses, the bottles being thrown out the back door, the glasses going into a half barrel of scummy water.

As the noise reduced to quiet talking, Mabry grabbed the shoulders of one of his two sons and pulled himself up, wincing as he did. Not to be stopped by a little pain, he held up his glass and yelled, "Here's to justice!"

The other men in the room held up their glasses and

drank. Then some young smart alec tossed his shot glass toward Marvin Bohn, and when he looked up, a couple more rannies hooted and threw theirs too, and the madder Bohn looked, the more glasses came flying at him, the men laughing and hooting. Glasses broke against the bar and the back bar, and the cannonade became so accurate, Bohn's derby went flying. He had to duck behind the bar until there was no more ammunition, and the men were all laughing and howling, crowding out into the street, happy as ants at a Sunday school picnic.

Mabry was half carried by his sons, and the Faulkner brothers were in the front along with them, as they went out into the middle of the street.

Opposite the mercantile, Mabry yelled, "Aufdemburg, you promised the twine, fetch it out!"

Aufdemburg got the message quick enough and came trotting out with two coils of fresh-cut sisal rope strong enough to hang a twelve-hundred-pound bull.

Ace and I moved along on the outskirts of the crowd, and lost Babe somewhere. I had the feeling Babe didn't want to see something that might give him bad dreams, and I thought that maybe he was smarter'n me in that respect.

One limber-legged Faulkner took the ropes, passed one over to a Mabry, and then commenced moving on down toward the jail.

"Bring 'em out, Witherspoon!" Bud Mabry yelled.

Marshal Witherspoon, followed by B. G. Hall and little Jake Levy, came out of the jail as if they'd been waiting to be summoned.

I noticed right off that even Witherspoon had taken off his guns, playing it safe.

"You can't have 'em!" Witherspoon yelled back, so's everybody could hear. "They get a fair trial!"

Women were moving in on the edges of the crowd along with Ace and me. They were craning their necks and standing on their toes to see, their little ones hanging on to their skirts as if to keep their mothers from flying away.

"Bring 'em out or we'll make a mess of your jail!" Mabry yelled back. "We won't wait!"

He was right. The sun was already setting and as soon as the desert night chill came down off the mountains, folks' tempers would cool down too.

"I'm the elected law here!" Witherspoon tried again. "You folks would commit murder if you hang these men!"

The Mabry and the Faulkner men were building their hangman's nooses.

"How many rounds?" young Mabry asked the older Faulkner.

"Must be thirteen," Faulkner said, crowding the rope loops around the main stem.

"They are innocent until proven guilty!" B. G. Hall yelled, waving his arms as if he was leading a brass band.

"Go back home and let the law take its course," Levy said like he was saying a memorized piece.

"You boys goin' to get tromped under the stompede!" Mabry yelled again. "Stand aside!"

As the Mabrys and Faulkners advanced, Witherspoon, Hall, and Levy moved away from the doorway.

"The key!" Mabry yelled.

"On the wall," Witherspoon muttered, looking at the ground.

There was an instant howl from the crowd. Even the women were screeching away as the leaders went inside, and the pitch of the hollering went higher and higher, peaking like a bunch of steam whistles when they dragged out Gibbon and Huerta.

Huerta was on his feet and his brown eyes were bugging out as he heard the screaming chorus and saw the number of people. Gibbon was in pain because the cowboys dragging him didn't worry about his wound.

He, too, looked as if he'd swallowed a bumblebee when he saw the numbers of people anxious to kill him. Plunging backwards, he tried to break loose, but he hadn't a chance.

Gibbon and Huerta were no longer old pals sharing their little jokes. They knew they were close to dying, and all of a sudden it was every man for himself.

Stubby Gibbon sized up the scene and started to cry, his weak chin bobbing up and down, tears coming from his little eyes.

Huerta was making his own plan, knowing he would never get any sympathy from a mob that would just as soon hang a Mexican for singing on Sunday.

"Boys, don't hang an innocent man!" Gibbon croaked out. "I've got a wife and four little tyker's over by Elko—they got nobody else but me!"

The crowd quieted down as Gibbon continued blubbering. "Four little towheaded tykers dependin' on me to feed 'em!" Gibbon bellowed and moaned.

The crowd seemed to feel sorry for him, but I had the notion they were baiting him along to see how well he could sing.

"My poor wife's expectin' another next month! She can't do for herself alone! Please! Don't come between me and those helpless chillern! Give me a chance!"

"What about my husband!" a hollow-cheeked woman yelled from right next to me. A stranger to me, she wore a homemade flannel dress, and her hands were red and knobby from plain hard work. "What chance did you give Sam Owensby!"

"Confess your crimes!" Bolivar Cromwell stepped forward, lifting his arm up, his index finger pointing toward the darkening sky.

"You might as well! You're goin' to be in hell shortly anyway!" Wade Filson roared.

"Wasn't my fault," Gibbon moaned, and as the crowd got all set to listen, Huerta jerked loose from his guards and ran back for the door of the jail, probably thinking he might pick up a gun and get out the back, but quick as he was, it still needed four long steps.

One of the Mabrys drew and shot him low in the back, so that he dropped instantly.

Before anybody else could fire, Marshal Witherspoon got in the way, his hands waving and him yelling, "No more! No more! There's women and children here!"

Doc Meredith came out of the crowd and leaned over the Mexican. Huerta's hands were clawing at the boardwalk, but nothing else was moving. He cried out a little shriek of pain every time he tried to take a breath.

Doc muttered something to Witherspoon, who relayed it in a loud voice back to the crowd. "He's hit in the lower spine. He's paralyzed from the hips down."

There was some discontented muttering about that.

The crowd didn't appreciate seeing a half-paralyzed man shrieking and clawing at the boardwalk like he wanted to crawl away to some hole to die.

"Get it over with!" a woman from the other side howled.

"What are you waitin' for?" another screamed.

The men didn't like that. You could see in their faces that next time they'd leave the womenfolk home.

"I'm innocent!" Gibbon appealed, but his moment had passed.

The crowd was tired of waiting and the men felt as if the women were taking over their show, and were feeling extra brutal because of it.

Bud Mabry weaved over to Gibbon and hit him in the crotch with an underslung right hand that doubled him up.

"Tie their hands!" Fly Swinner yelled.

"Where's a tree?"

Hell, there wasn't a tree in town. Nobody'd thought of it before. Now they were becoming divided and fractious.

"Damnit," someone mumbled next to me, "this town can't even hang a man right."

I looked around and saw it was Ace, his mouth twisted, his face pale.

"The hay tree!" somebody yelled.

"Let's go!"

Yes, there was what they called the hay tree, which was a walnut log projecting from the second-story peak of the livery barn. It had a pulley and a long rope that was used to haul hay up to the haymow for storing, and it'd serve for hanging two small men.

The Mexican screamed when the men picked him up by the shoulders and dragged his limp legs along, his big roweled spurs snagging in the dirt and popping loose.

With his hands tied behind his back, Gibbon started yelling, "I only did what I was told to do!" but nobody paid any attention to him. His yelling covered the change of scene from Main Street over to the show at the livery barn, like a curtain covers up the change of scenery when a troupe comes through doing *Uncle Tom's Cabin*.

"He said he'd hurt my little babes if I didn't do it!" Gibbon howled, but everyone was moving and expected him to say about anything he could now.

"Bring out a couple horses!" Mabry yelled.

I'll be damned if some fool didn't lead out my Buck.

I crowded through, limping and yelling, "Goddamnit to hell! No!"

No one paid me any attention 'til I got to my horse and grabbed the lead rope out of some farmer's hand.

Then everybody laughed because I was so mad, and the clodhopper so bewildered.

I led Buck back into the sweet-smelling shadows of the barn whilst they fetched out a workhorse and a mustang that nobody cared about, and I stood in the doorway as Mabrys and Faulkners slung their ropes up over the hay tree.

The men moved quickly, setting Gibbon up bareback on the fat old draft horse and the Mexican onto the broomtail, when somebody else yelled, "Tie their legs together so they don't kick!"

"How the hell you goin' to hang 'em if they're tied on a damn horse!" Mabry yelled back, getting madder and madder as the time worked by.

Some rannies held the Mexican up on the mustang, and the nooses were put over the men's heads, the knots adjusted under their ears, and the bitter ends tied off on a stanchion.

"It was Turnbull's doin'! Beecher Turnbull! He paid for it! Fifty dollars a head!" Gibbon yelled.

Huerta was quiet but his lips were moving and I figured he was saying his Hail Marys as fast as he could.

"You all heard that!" Mex Abrams burst out to the front of the crowd and raised his arm up righteously. "You all heard him name Turnbull as the guilty party!"

Nobody said "Ready, set, go" or "Do you have any last words?"; not even B. G. Hall had time to make a long prayer to Our Father Which Art in Heaven, because right on the banker's heels came burly Metta Snapp bulling her way through.

Shouldering past the Faulkners and Mabrys, she lifted her furled-up umbrella and swatted the butt of the fat horse, who didn't move at first; but he felt the second one and walked forward a couple of steps, leaving Dee Gibbon dangling by the neck, his legs kicking wildly.

Half a second later she brought the umbrella down on the rump of the mustang, and he jumped right off. The Mexican's neck snapped, and as he jerked back over the butt, the little mustang kicked him in his bleeding belly with both hind hooves, then bolted down the street.

The hush was instant and profound in the orange twilight.

The only noise was Gibbon gargling. The only motion was him swinging on the new rope, kicking and swinging.

Small as he was, Gibbon's weight and gyrations still stretched the new rope and the crowd stood awestruck as the toes of his boots touched the dirt and horse manure;

he was still gargling, his face red, but not blue like the Mexican's, his neck muscles ridged out to hold back the bite of the noose.

As he swung back, his toes touched the ground again, and he struggled to find some footing.

Bud Mabry, held up between his two sons, looked puzzled as the rope stretched bit by bit and Gibbon continued to live.

"Hang him again!" somebody yelled.

"He's been hung once! That's all the law allows!" somebody else yelled.

"Let him loose! He's paid the price!" a woman called out.

"I'll be goddamned if I do," Mabry roared, and staggering free from his boys, threw his arms around Gibbon's shoulders, throwing his own weight against the rope.

There was a long moment as the heavyset ranchman hugged Gibbon close, stretching his head farther and farther away from his body until the neck bones snapped. No matter that by now Gibbon's boots settled flat-footed on the ground, the hanging was done.

I heard the hollow-cheeked Mrs. Sam Owensby moan, "Oh, my Lord, no!" and I thought it was a little late for the lady to change her mind.

11

A SMALL RIDER ON A LONG-LEGGED CHESTNUT GELDING came into the street from the west at a gallop. Reining the foam-slopped horse down to a quick trot, he passed on east before anyone realized they'd never seen him before. Such an event in normal times would have kept the town buzzing with gossip for a week, but right then, the town fathers were haggling about the burials.

B. G. Hall took charge of the bodies once Aufdemburg, Bohn, Crawford, Levy, and Pedragal agreed to stand good for the expenses.

"Nothing fancy," Marvin Bohn said. "They're as dead as they will ever be."

"Just a pine box, that's all. Fly will dig the hole for a couple of drinks," Mex Abrams said, "and I guess you can say a prayer if folks think it'll help clear up the stink."

"Why should my prayer come free?" B. G. Hall protested. "Do you loan money without interest?"

"Save the prayer then," Frank Pedragal said. "That pair's in hell already."

141

The women waited over at Aufdemburg's store because there wasn't any other place for victims of natural disasters, such as floods, sandstorms, locusts, or mass craziness.

They'd wait there until the men rehashed the hanging a few more times and got their stomachs settled, then they'd start for home in the dark.

Normally, caught out late at night like that, they'd camp in the lot next to the livery barn, sleeping either in or under their wagons, but no one wanted to go near Dad Crawford's livery, especially as Huerta and Gibbon were still hanging there, pending a deal with B. G. Hall.

"Two dollars apiece for the boxes and two for you to load 'em up. That's six dollars. You don't want it, we'll turn the whole mess over to Fly," Jake Levy said.

Over at the other end of the bar, Dag Petersen was laughing. "Boil me for a snappin' turtle, I never seen a woman whip a horse like old lady Snapp!"

"Likely ruined that umbrella," Wayne Farnhorst snorted.

"How come she got her nose into our business?" Wade Filson glowered around, angry at about everything and everybody. "It wasn't her affair."

"I guess she got tired of waiting," Tuck Krendel offered as an explanation.

"It don't set right with me," Wade argued. "By damn, she didn't even let Gibbon finish his last words."

"Maybe because Gibbon was tryin' to lay the blame onto Turnbull," Mexican Abrams said.

"Somethin' to that, all right," Dag Petersen said, swaying from the waist up from two days of heavy fighting with John Barleycorn.

"That's the truth." Wayne Farnhorst banged on the bar. "By God, she wasn't bein' merciful, she was shuttin' up Gibbon is what she was doin'."

"I heard him plain as day sayin' it was Turnbull hired 'em to do his dirty work," Ed Lewis added loudly, attracting the others, who were willing enough to forgo the dirty feelings we all felt.

"Why, sure, Gibbon was telling us how Turnbull hired him, and then what do you know? Turnbull's woman stompedes the horses and stops him from talkin'!" Wade Filson roared.

"Hold on a minute! Did you say that murdering Gibbon confessed and named Turnbull?"

Bud Mabry staggered forward into the light, his eyes red and half asleep, his face stubbled with a week's growth of beard, and his hat tipped back on his head. You'd think if somebody tapped him on the shoulder, he'd fall down, he looked so tired.

"That's the God's truth!" Wayne Farnhorst smacked the bar again with the palm of his hand. "I heard him say it!"

"How else you think he was makin' all that money?" Mexican Abrams slipped his mischief into the palaverin'. "Wasn't he workin' for Turnbull all the way through?"

"You're sayin' that Beecher Turnbull is just as guilty as Gibbon and the Mex," Bolivar Cromwell boomed out.

"Let's hang that stump-sucker!" Mabry grated slowly, a word at a time.

"You notice he wasn't anywhere around when we did up his hired hands." Tuck Krendel had to put in his nickel's worth.

"You goin' to take the word of a scalawag like Gibbon?" B. G. Hall interrupted, still sore from being beat down on his mortician's price.

"Somethin' to that," Marvin Bohn said, his flat face beginning to show a sort of contempt for all of us. "He'd say anythin' with a rope around his neck."

"There's somethin' damn strange about his wife and brother disappearin'," Mex Abrams countered Bohn's statement.

"It just happens I know that Beecher Turnbull cut

Gibbon off the payroll a month ago," Doc Meredith said clearly into the confused, surly crowd.

"Why'd he do that?" Wade Filson wanted to know.

"I understand Wes finally beat the truth into his head. He figured they'd gone too far."

The men nodded thoughtfully, because it made sense.

"How'd you know that, Doc?" Bud Mabry's head tolled slowly back and forth.

"I know," Doc said, not backing down.

"Then why would they kill Pat Faulkner?"

"Maybe they were rustlin' his beef. Maybe they figured to make more trouble for Turnbull," Doc said. "Why don't everybody go to bed and sleep it off?"

"How come you're stickin' your big beak in this?" Mex Abrams stepped forward, facing Doc. "He payin' you, too?"

"Your piles are gettin' worse from carryin' so much money around, Abrams," Doc retorted sharply, like a terrier marking his territory.

Abrams flushed and said, "We ought to get this all cleared up so's we can get on with our business."

"Why don't we go up there and talk to him?" Wade Filson put in.

"You think he'd tell you the truth?" Abrams sneered.

"If he fired those two for takin' a shot at me, I'd like to know it," I said.

Abrams tried to stare me down, and the others started mumbling around until Bud Mabry got his head up and growled blearily, "Let's go hang that stump-sucker!"

"We ain't goin' to hang nobody more tonight!" Bolivar Cromwell boomed out. "You want to go up and talk to Turnbull, I'll lead the way, but not if you're bent on more killin'."

"Let's go." Mabry looked dully around at his boys and the Faulkner men, who were outsiders for the most part.

144

"Let's go!" Wade Filson yelled, and lighted a coal oil lantern.

Other lanterns were fired up and, with Marvin Bohn shaking his head in disgust, the group staggered out, found their ponies, and started up the street toward the big house.

Hardly had they gotten started than Marshal Witherspoon came out into the street with his own bull's-eye lantern and yelled, "What's goin' on here?"

"We're goin' up to talk with Beecher Turnbull," Bolivar Cromwell answered loud enough for all to hear. "We're peaceable. We want to know if he fired that pair of coyotes a month ago like Doc says."

"I'm coming along, and I'll make damned sure it's peaceable, too," Witherspoon said angrily. He'd had about enough hiding for the day, and looked to be set on a hair trigger.

Witherspoon took the lead alongside Bolivar Cromwell and as we came up to the house, we could see there were no lamps lighted and the whole place was as quiet as a treeful of doll rags.

"Maybe he's gone out to the ranch," Bolivar suggested.

"Make some noise," Bud Mabry said, spurring his horse forward.

Suddenly everyone was too timid to even call out to the house, and Bud Mabry cussed some, then hauled out his .44 and fired twice toward the moon. The noise and flame stilled the crowd even more, and some turned in the darkness and commenced walking their ponies back down the dark road.

No lamps were lighted, no doors or windows were opened.

"Nobody there," Bolivar Cromwell said, dismounting and marching up the broad steps to the porch.

He banged the brass knocker and yelled, "Anybody home?"

"He's run," Bud Mabry said thickly, hardly able to talk. "Gone scat."

"Likely off on business," Doc said.

Abrams tried the door and it swung open wide. He looked back at us, and said, "Come on, maybe he's hiding. Beecher Turnbull!" he yelled into the house. "Come on out!"

After a short wait, he moved into the hall. I followed the rest of them, my leg not feeling anything one way or another anymore. We tramped through the living room parlor and through the study.

"He's hidin' somewhere," Abrams said, and led the way up the stairs to the bedrooms, and everybody looked in while he checked the closets and under the beds. Most everyone was so stunned at being inside the big house like burglars, they were tiptoeing and wishing they'd never come.

Abrams went ahead and opened the door to the big bedroom. Holding his lantern high, he and Witherspoon looked through the elegant rooms, with the same results. No doubt about it—Beecher Turnbull was gone.

Witherspoon shone his bull's-eye into the fireplace, then poked through the ashes. Gradually the crowd followed into the room, sniffing at vanished perfume and eyeing the featherbeds and down quilts.

Witherspoon came over and pulled back the counterpane, revealing a pillow with a smear of dried blood. He lifted the pillow, and we all saw the gold cuff links and the cameo brooch. Someone said, "Those cuff links are Dan Turnbull's."

Nobody needed to say who owned the brooch.

"Turnbull killed them and now he's run for it," Witherspoon said heavily, "that's all there is to it."

I'd taken so many low blows in the past couple of days, this one didn't hurt so much. Maybe someday I would be out somewhere where there was a green meadow and a little clear-running stream, and I'd think about that blue-eyed girl who should have been mine. I would think of her playing in the grass and giggling, and maybe, if I was far enough away, I could blubber and beller. But not now and not here. There was too much of the lynch stink in this room, too much greed and envy and simple blood lust for violent death.

"He might make it to Mexico, but likely he'd ride on over the mountains to California," Dad Crawford guessed.

"It won't do no good riding out in the night without some kind of trail," Marshal Witherspoon said, which put most everyone's mind at ease, because of the down-pulling weariness that had replaced all the fiery preparations for the hanging. Men were stumbling with leaden feet and bleary eyes, me included, and when I saw how it was going, I got Ed Lewis by the arm and said, "I'm goin' to get some sleep."

"We'll catch the sonofabitch tomorrow," Bud Mabry said.

"Everybody meet in the street at daybreak," Mex Abrams called out. "We'll show him a thing or two about runnin' away!"

On our way to the Lewises' rooming house, I noticed Marvin Bohn had locked his doors and blown out the lamps, so there'd be no more forty rod this night.

B. G. Hall, now that things were settling down, had loaded Gibbon and Huerta on his black lumber wagon, and would have the pair underground quick enough, and likely he'd pocket the four dollars that was supposed to go for the coffins.

Him and Fly would work it out before dawn and nobody'd be the wiser.

My leg was starting to burn, but it'd be better with some rest, and I argued with myself as to whether to go out to the ranch in the morning or go with the posse after Beecher Turnbull.

Sleep overtook me before the argument was settled, and the fate of Beecher Turnbull became completely unimportant.

I did have a vision of Jean Louise, but this time her

face had lost its vivacity and youth, her skin had lost its glow, and the sparkling, mischievous light was gone from her eyes. It was more like a painted portrait of somebody that had been gathering dust and smoke fumes and flyspecks for a long time. It was the portrait of a dead person by a dead artist.

I sure appreciate knowin' you, Wesley . . .

Morning came cold sober and hung over for most of the town. I felt good enough except for the knitting needles working my leg. I decided to have breakfast down at Ed's Cafe and figure what my plans were after I'd had a cup of coffee.

The restaurant was almost full, which was unusual this early in the morning, and even before I'd had my coffee, I'd decided I'd go along and see the cards played out.

Bud Mabry was sitting at the counter trying not to cradle his head in his hands. Dad Crawford was pouring a shot of clear alcohol into Bud's coffee mug, then into his own. They looked like a scruffy crew of cutthroats and grub line riders, instead of hardworking cattlemen.

I wondered if I looked that bad.

Marshal Witherspoon turned up. His wife had cooked him a decent breakfast, but he still looked a hundred years old. On the one hand he was sick because he'd given his prisoners over to the mob without a fight, and on the other hand he was mad enough to be damned sure Mabry and Abrams and the rest of the sly ones didn't take over again.

Didn't make a nevermind to me. I didn't want to boss nothing. I believed Doc's story about that pair being fired after shootin' at me, and I held no grudge against Turnbull.

As for his wife and brother, I'd decided I'd rather wait and see.

I thought about going out and helping Red, but then I'd never get the straight of it, not from any of these folks, who could hardly figure what day it was and which end of a horse eats.

After a breakfast of ham and eggs and flapjacks, the day looked a little brighter.

The men gathered outside on the boardwalk, waiting for someone to tell them what to do.

I went out and leaned on the hitch rail while they palavered about which way to go.

"Hunger Pass is clear of snow now; likely he's passed over that way," Wade Filson said, but not with the fire he'd had the day before.

"If it was me and I had his money, I'd be halfway to Mexico by now," Wayne Farnhorst said.

"And you might die of thirst, too, if you don't know the water holes," Jacob Levy said.

"Why don't we play it safe and send somebody out to the ranch headquarters and make sure he ain't hiding out there?"

"Could be he's forted up out there with his cowhands backin' him up," Dad Crawford said, nodding wisely and gumming his rubbery lips together.

"Then we better all go together," Bolivar Cromwell boomed out. "Hell, it's only three miles."

"That's better'n ridin' for thirty up in them mountains," Tuck Krendel added on his advice, and, at last, with a definite place to go, the scraggly bunch of riders found their horses and mounted up.

Piles or no piles, Mex Abrams mounted up on a padded saddle.

Marshal Witherspoon said, "We ain't goin' in shooting. We ain't going for a hanging. We are going to find out what happened, and then we'll go legal from there. Understood?"

There was a grumbling of agreement from men with aching heads and queasy stomachs.

Witherspoon kneed his big bay gelding into an easy trot down the street until he hit the trail that ran from the big house out east over the flats to the ranch headquarters.

This time of the year, except for sagebrush, the forage is mostly gone, and we raised up a column of reddish dust as we rode over the plain.

"Keep an eye out for sign!" Witherspoon hollered.

"What're we lookin' for?" somebody called back.

"Tracks. Spare clothes. Papers. Jewelry. Could be anything," Witherspoon called.

I figured he was right; the way the clothes and stuff had been burned, it wouldn't be much of a surprise to see some of it scattered along the way.

We found nothing untoward out there on the treeless plain, only wagon ruts, deeply ground cattle trails, and a spooked jackrabbit. Approaching the ranch, there were more cattle scattered about, and among the loose horses I recognized the good roan stud we'd let loose from our trap a few weeks before. He'd found some more mares loose or he'd fought another stud for them.

I didn't see any brands on the mares, and judging from their wildness and general conformation, they were mustangs, free for the taking.

Witherspoon pulled us down to a trot as we approached the ranchstead, where the bunkhouse, cook house, barn, sheds, and corrals were clustered by a good spring that fed a little stream for a while until it disappeared underground again.

Coming to the first corral, which held a few sleepy cayuses, Witherspoon pulled up and yelled, "Hello, the ranch!"

A big fat black man came out of the cook house and looked over our way and then looked back over his shoulder at the country beyond. "Come on in," he yelled, like he knew he didn't have any choice in the matter and so why did the Lord put him down here in this useless spot.

Witherspoon moved the bay forward until he faced the big black man on the steps of the cook house.

"What you folks want?"

"We want to talk to Turnbull," Witherspoon said clearly, his eyes fixed on the black man's round face.

"He not here. He didn't come out this morning."

"Where's the crew?"

"Off yonder at the little Daisy line camp. They all over there gatherin' up some beef cattle Mr. Turnbull sold."

Witherspoon eyed him steadily, saying nothing.

"Beggin' your pardon if I overspoke myself . . . what you folks want?" the black cook asked again in a little voice.

"Turnbull," Witherspoon said. "I'm going to count three, and if you don't tell me where he is, I'm going to send you to hell in a basket. One—"

"Oh, Lawdy," he started jabbering, "may my head blossom for the grave, I don't know. It ain't my job. I's cluttered with troubles . . ."

"Two—"

"Better go talk to Mr. Elam Pinnick, the foreman . . . less'n I overspoke myself, he don't know neither. I swear, I wish I was home and sick in bed . . ." His eyes rolled up like china saucers.

"Steady down. I believe you," Witherspoon said quietly, "but, listen—if you're lying, I'll see you eat your own *huevos,* understand?"

"Sir, I understand—and I'm overly beholden to you, but the fact is he didn't ride out this morning, and from the poisoned look of him, he's likely got took down dead. I swear it's too much wrath and cabbage for this old darky!"

"Back to town," Witherspoon barked, and wheeled the bay around.

Going at an easy gallop, we could see the big house perched on the bluff like an old-time castle, and on beyond it the dusty boxes of Buttonwillow.

Buck was feeling good to be out of the barn, and my leg preferred riding to walking. Thinking it over, I pretty much decided to go back out to the ranch and get washed clean of this pack of coyotes.

The men looked as if they were ready to give it up and go back to minding their own business. Tired, hung over, dirty with the sweat of a lynching that would take a lot of scrubbing to wash off, confused as to where they might have to go, they looked like they would just as soon go on home and let Marshal Witherspoon run down Turnbull and find out where he'd buried the bodies.

We trooped back into Buttonwillow and tied up in front of the Prince Albert. Most felt a glass of beer would help to settle their stomachs and quiet the tom-toms banging in their heads.

I noticed Red standing in the doorway of Aufdemburg's Mercantile, and thought, well, now I don't have to decide nothing. I turned in there to put Buck at the hitch rail.

Red came down the step and met me on the board-walk.

"I guess your leg will ride, Nez."

"I'm ready soon as you're ready."

"I ain't ready," he said so quietly nobody could hear him. "That Turnbull came by last night. He needed a change of horses and I traded him the sorrel. He give me a hundred dollars to boot."

"Hell, that old sorrel ain't worth that much money," I said, leading him down the boardwalk away from people.

"His black's a better horse," Red nodded, "but he was worn out and the man was in a hurry."

"Which way did he go from there?"

"Northwest. I followed his tracks. He was heading for Hunger Pass."

"What do you think?" I asked.

"He's nothin' to me."

"Me neither, now that I know I'm not marked for dry-gulchin'."

"Don't want revenge?" Red looked at me closely, as if I was a spice cake that wasn't turning out right in the oven.

"Too late," I said, shaking my head.

"I'd like a piece of Melba Lauder's cherry pie, if there's any left," Red murmured.

I thought, well, that's it. I fell in and out of love without ever hardly saying a mumbling word to the lady when she was alive.

That's the way Wesley Bengard is with women. Take 'em or leave 'em, no worries. There's always another one on the next stage, and they all look gray at night.

I sure appreciate knowin' you, Wesley.

"C'mon, Wes," he said, and started off toward Ed's Cafe.

I was set to follow when a pair of riders came dusting into town from the west. They both carried saddlebags and bedrolls tied behind their saddles and they didn't belong to any cattle outfit in the Juniper.

The lean, orange-haired one in front saw Witherspoon's brass badge and reined over immediately. His face was burned about as red as his hair, and his eyes were almost colorless.

"You the law hereabouts?"

"What's the trouble?" Witherspoon said as he nodded.

"Nothin' much, I guess. Some jasper tried stealin' my horse this mornin' early."

"You know him?"

"I do now," the red-faced waddy chuckled. "He was a big tree, but I chopped him down some."

"Dressed pretty nice, in town clothes?" Witherspoon asked carefully.

"That's him. Big man, but gone to fat. Rode a winded sorrel."

"Whereabouts was this?"

"Just down this side of Hunger Pass. It's open now."

"You're sayin' he's afoot up in the pass right now?"

"He is unless he can find another horse." The saddle tramp nodded cheerily. "You know him?"

"We're looking for him."

"Better be careful," the cowboy said, "we didn't find his guns."

= 12 =

H E MUST'VE GOT LOST IN THE DARK," RED SAID. "WENT too far south, then found our place and figured out where he was."

"He'd've done better to stay home and act innocent," I said. "Now they know he's guilty."

"Guilty of what?" Red asked, looking away.

"Murdering his wife and kid brother," I answered, but with some doubts.

"Seems like a big bite to swallow."

"He had a temper and he's strong as a bull."

"Bodies?"

"No," I said, and explained about the burned things.

"Everything except bodies," Red nodded. "You can hang an Indian for less, but not Mr. Beecher Turnbull."

"Ready, boys?" Witherspoon called out. "It's no more'n twenty miles straight across. We can bring him back by dark."

There was a muttering of dissent. Most of the remaining riders had had enough. Twenty miles across the flat plain and then climbing up the bad trail of Hunger Pass wasn't impossible, but it wasn't all that attractive either.

"I'll put up a reward, boys," Mex Abrams yelled out. "Five hundred dollars dead or alive for the murderin' bastard!"

That did it. The posse yipped and hollered, and drowned out Witherspoon, who was trying to say he wanted Turnbull alive.

After a minute he decided he'd settle it later and that the time to move was right now, while he still had a posse that would follow him.

I looked at Red and nodded.

"Might as well see it through," he said and climbed aboard a heavy-shouldered roan. "We won't have any fun in Mexico if you don't know the worst for sure."

I didn't argue. Likely he was right as usual.

We kept to the side and upwind to avoid the dust, and rode along at the steady canter Witherspoon set for us. He understood how much a horse could do and couldn't do, and there was no way you could race pell-mell across that plain and hold it for twenty miles. So it was canter and walk, canter and walk, cavalry style, and the horses adjusted to it after a while so they stayed warm but didn't suffer from the heaves or heat stroke.

The country was empty except for small, brittle, dry coyote brush and the weathered brown grass. The sun would burn your eyes out if you didn't have your hat brim just over your nose, and if you didn't know there was water at the foot of the mountains, you'd give up and go back.

Saddle gear creaked, horses snorted and rattled, but the riders were quiet, not so much like they were grim avenging angels, but more like a hard-used group of country men that have set their mind on doin' something.

In all there was an even dozen of us. The Faulkners had gone home, figuring they'd paid off the debt to Pat, and most of the Mabrys had gone back to their ranches with the same idea. Bud's two young sons were still with him, making sure he could set the saddle, but except for them and me and Red, the others were from town: B. G. Hall, Bolivar Cromwell, Witherspoon, Wayne Damker, Ed Lewis, Wade Filson, Frank Pedragal, and E. Micklesen Abrams.

"Ought to be enough to dog down one man afoot," I said to Red.

"People like the catch," Red nodded.

"He won't be easy."

"I hope he didn't ruin the sorrel. I shouldn't have sold him."

"That sorrel will be all right, but he's too long legged for mountain travel."

It seemed like the longer we rode, the farther away the mountains moved, until we came to a brushy creek that lay in the first shadows of the rocky bulwark.

We stopped to water the horses, but we'd brought nothing to eat, and weren't of a mind to waste more time.

Witherspoon led us on up the gulch of the creek, which we all knew was supposed to be a trail over the mountains, even though most of the time it was a boulder-strewn streambed, sometimes dry, sometimes wet, but never running hard at this time of the year.

On over the pass, another similar kind of streambed sloped down toward the foothills of California, where you'd cut a well-used north and south wagon road that would take you in to Roseville and Auburn and then Sacramento. From there you could take a railroad, stage, or steamboat anywhere you wanted to go.

The horses hated the loose cobbles and slippery, water-worn bedrock, but it wasn't like they were galloping. Now it was plain hard uphill walking.

They slipped and stumbled, but none fell, and after an hour of it, they began to catch the fever of the hunt again. We all were watching for tracks cutting off from the streambed, but it was steep on either side, and it looked to me as if he was penned in.

He couldn't go down, so he had to be on up yonder somewhere, maybe holed up with that big .38-55 Winchester resting on a rock and aiming right down on us.

For sure he couldn't miss.

"That sonofabitch will pay double for makin' it so damned hard," Bud Mabry growled when Marshal Witherspoon called for a rest on a green knoll just out of the gulch.

"I'm goin' to take my pay in Mex's reward money," Wade Filson said.

"Not if I beat you to it," Frank Pedragal put in, his fine mustache looking bristly from the past couple of days.

"I'm not givin' the bushwhacker a chance at me," Ed Lewis said, patting an old long-barreled .45-70 Springfield sticking out of his boot. "I can take him before he even knows we're onto him."

"We're not onto him yet," Witherspoon growled, "and I want no shootin' unless I say so."

Lewis winked at me and said, "Yes, sir, Colonel Witherspoon. Thy will be done."

"You boys just remember the state ranger will be coming into Buttonwillow late today or tomorrow. You show him a back-shot, oozy corpse, you're going to be visiting the judge in Carson."

"Maybe he'll be too heavy to haul back. Maybe BG can bury him under a pile of rocks, and we can let it go at that," Wayne Farnhorst said, trying to look shrewd.

"I can handle this alone if you boys think you're going to a turkey shoot," Witherspoon growled.

"I come this far," I said, "and I'd as liefer hear his side of it."

"You takin' his side?" Mex Abrams come back at me, trying to act like I was his hired hand.

"I'm on Witherspoon's side this time," I said, getting some riled at the pissants peckin' away at me. "I sure ain't goin' to help you move out Beecher Turnbull so you can take over."

Before he could come back at me, Witherspoon interrupted, "That's enough. Let's go on up and get it over with."

He kicked his horse back to the trail and we commenced climbing up the winding canyon again, with nothing any more settled than before, but with tempers close to fighting mad, and no love lost between us.

Maybe Witherspoon wanted it that way, thinking he could control us better, but he wasn't reckoning on how salty we all felt from lack of sleep and chasing around doing things we had no experience in doing.

When I thought that it took Metta Snapp to whip up those two horses, I felt like hanging my head in shame.

Another mile and we came on to Burleigh's Flat, where a prospector had built a log shack too far back to remember.

Folks had quit using it after the varmints moved into it, but they'd camp outside because there was grass and a clear brook full of snow water.

Beyond the cabin our long-legged sorrel grazed with its ears cocked our way.

"That's your brand, ain't it?" Bud Mabry asked me.

"Dad—" his son said, trying to caution him.

"It's ours," I agreed, about to explain it, but it struck me all of a sudden that he'd used his bully tone of voice on me.

"You give it to him?" Mabry snarled at me like I was his cub.

I drove Buck forward hard, shoving his shoulder up against Mabry's bay with my right hand clear, and when I had him face to face, eye to eye, I said, "Yes."

I'da killed him just then I was so mad at the pissy-assed polecats raggin' away all the time.

He turned the bay, mumbling, "All right . . ."

I watched him in case he drew on me off to my side, but Red had him pegged, and he didn't like the idea of a crossfire.

"You don't have to be so damned salty," he grumbled, "I only asked."

"I don't answer to you, Mabry," I said plain out, and waited for him to pick it up, but he wouldn't.

"That's enough!" Marshal Witherspoon rode across between us. "We got better things to do than bicker about a damned horse. Is that the one he was ridin'?" he asked Red instead of me.

"It's his horse," Red said, which you could take to mean it wasn't our horse anymore, or any way you wanted to.

"Likely he's gone afoot on up the canyon," Wade Filson said. "He won't be far."

"Might be he cut over to Bee Camp," Frank Pedragal said, showing he knew more about the country than any of the rest of us.

"Where's that?" Witherspoon frowned.

"About eight miles north and west. A trail comes into it from the California side."

"Light down, boys," Witherspoon said. "Make a circle and look for his tracks."

Ed Lewis had the rifle out, scanning over its long barrel at the high ground. "I'd sure like to catch him out in the open . . ."

"What've you got against him?" I asked quietly.

"Same as everybody else. The big blowhard keeps tryin' to step on us like we was bugs."

I looked at Lewis's thin, ratty features and shifty eyes. He liked to prowl at night, and the next thing to night prowling is peeking through windows. A thought flashed through my head that he had seen Jean Louise maybe getting ready for bed and had a case on her, in a way like me, except all the peekin' I ever did was inside my own head.

We left Bolivar Cromwell to watch the horses while we bowlegged it, with Red in the lead, slowly around the edge of the grassy swale, keeping next to the timber. The ground was still soft from the snowmelt so you could see deer tracks and one good-sized bear's tracks, but nobody in boots had crossed from the grass into the woods.

"He's up canyon," Red said as we came back to the main trail.

"We had to look," Witherspoon said.

Then I thought he had used that walk around to cool down the tempers of tired men, including me.

Mounting up again, we left the red horse to graze, and I thought we'd pick him up on the way back if he wasn't windbroke and bottomed out.

"Hell—maybe he picked up another horse somewhere and is over the pass and halfway to Auburn by now," one of Mabry's sons said.

"I can't spend all my time ridin' the damned hills," complained Frank Pedragal. "Somebody's got to earn a livin'."

"If we don't catch him before the top, we'll give it up," Witherspoon said.

"We don't have any legal right to arrest a man in California anyways," Bolivar Cromwell declared.

"He'll have to come back someday," B. G. Hall said. "A man can't let a lifetime's work go by just like that."

"He can if he's goin' to get hung for it," Mex Abrams said, like his mind was already on how he could transfer Turnbull's property over into his name.

I figured he'd work it out soon enough.

Riding alongside Red, I noticed his eyes were looking on up the canyon.

The rocky trail made a slow turn to the north and the streambed was more of a series of low ledges like granite steps rising toward the pass.

Red set his jaw and shook his head, not pleased with himself.

I didn't look up. I knew Red had seen him, but I was going to let somebody else sing out.

"There's the sonofabitch," Ed Lewis murmured, as if he was afraid his quarry would hear him. He slid off his dun mare with the rifle and moved to a slab of rock.

"Five hundred dollars says you can't do it," Mex Abrams said softly.

"That on top of the reward?" Ed Lewis asked, putting the stock to his cheek and lining up on the distant little spot of gray clambering up the trail.

Turnbull was near the top and paying no attention to his back trail. As near as I could see he wasn't carrying a rifle.

"Sure," Abrams replied quickly.

"Hold it!" Witherspoon yelled, but there was nothing he could do because he was too far ahead and too many riders were in between.

I could see Ed Lewis squint and his finger curl around the trigger, and silently cussing myself for bein' a damn fool, I threw my hat in his face just as he squeezed.

Whether it was the hat or his unsteady hand that made him miss, it didn't make any difference. The bullet went wide, and he glared up at me with dirty hate fixed in the tight lines of his face.

"Why the hell?"

"Marshal said hold it." I leaned over and fetched my hat from the rock.

"I had him dead to rights!" he came back, red hot.

"It don't pay to backshoot a man long range."

"You're so holy?" Abrams snapped at me.

"Better you ride back to your bank, Abrams," I said, "because you're goin' to talk yourself into an early grave out here."

"I'm stayin', cowboy," he gritted, "and, mister, you're leavin' Juniper country."

I flipped out my .44 and stuck the barrel in his hollow cheek, crowding the buckskin closer to him so he couldn't back off. "Say that again, you rotten bloodsucker!"

His eyes were turned down, trying to see my hand, and I was mad enough just then to drive lightning through his head.

"I'm sorry, Bengard," he said. "I apologize . . ."

Letting off, I holstered the Colt. "Get it straight. I'm backin' the Marshal's play."

"Steady on, Wes," Bolivar Cromwell came back. "I know how you feel."

"I've had a bellyful of this horseshit!" Witherspoon came charging back. "By God, Abrams, you and Mabry and Lewis and anybody else bent on legal murder better, by God, head back down the road, because this time you're going to do it my way!"

"You mean I rode up here all the way to kiss that sonofabitch's ass?" Mabry yelled.

I looked up at the distant figure in gray and saw that he had stopped climbing and was looking back down at us. He'd heard the shot and maybe the ricochet and was trying to figure out what he should do next.

He only had two or three hundred yards to go to cross over the pass, and we couldn't ride up that broken rock fast enough to catch him. The whole thing boiled down to whether we could shoot him on the way.

For him, I could see he had no choice. He had to keep running, no matter what. Remembering the lynching of the night before, he couldn't take a chance on our being peaceable, especially after Lewis had taken his shot.

Turning back to the rocky path, the gray-clad figure commenced scrabbling up the trail again.

"He's goin' to go free," Abrams said. "Is that what you want?"

"No. I want to take him back to Buttonwillow alive," Witherspoon yelled. "Goddamnit, how many times I got to say it!"

"While you're talkin' he's gettin' clear," Mabry taunted him. "The man that paid Gibbon. The man that murdered his wife and brother, and you're afraid to hurt him a little!"

Witherspoon, red in the face, turned his horse, cupped his hand to his mouth, and yelled up at the fleeing figure.

"Turnbull . . . ! Want . . . to . . . talk . . ."

"He ain't goin' to wait," Mabry said, disgusted.

Witherspoon glanced over his shoulder and noticed what I'd missed. "Where's Lewis?"

The sneaky little coyote had drifted off out of sight.

Right then I knew there was no help for it. The iron had been in the forge a long time, and now it was cherry red hot and ready for the hammer.

In that moment, Turnbull turned at the very top so he was skylighted between Nevada and California. He cupped his hands and yelled, "Back . . . later . . . later . . ."

The Springfield went off with a boom that made its own echo so that the canyon was sending back "later . . . boom . . . later . . . boom . . . later . . . boom . . ." and we sat our saddles watching the gray-clad figure cave in on his right side. Saw him go to a kneeling position, try to catch himself with his left leg, but the 450-grain slug had too much powder behind it and mashed him over on his side. He was still trying to claw at the rock with his hands, but the heavy weight of his body dragged him back down the slope.

"Come on!" Witherspoon spurred his bay on up the trail as Lewis came back from his covert yelling, the long-barreled Springfield lifted high.

"I got him, by God, Abrams! I got him for you!"

I kicked Buck on Witherspoon's tail and we reached Beecher Turnbull at about the same time.

Sitting on the ground with his back to a rock, a pool of blood spreading out from his right knee, Turnbull's face was a dirty white from the shock, but the expressions of anger and hatred crossing back and forth over his heavy features were like thunderheads over the desert.

I tied a leather strap around his upper leg and shut off the bleeding, and Witherspoon looked through Turnbull's pocket for a gun, but he was unarmed.

"Bastardly backshootin' sonsabitches—" Turnbull said, looking up at us, then clamped his wide mouth shut.

Smiling, B. G. Hall, always ready with a knife, slit open the gray worsted pants leg past the knee and bent over the wound.

I could see the bullet had smacked the knee, busted it

to pieces, and Turnbull would be a cripple for the rest of his life.

B. G. Hall drew the pants leg down over the mess and for once he had nothing to say.

"Most unfortunate," Bolivar Cromwell said, shaking his head.

"The bastard deserved it," Mabry said, unsmiling.

Turnbull looked us over, saw the rifle in Ed Lewis's hands, jabbed a finger at him, then at Mabry, then, passing by me and Red, at Mex Abrams.

"You'll pay," he muttered, then nodded his head and closed his eyes.

"What happened to your wife and brother?" Witherspoon asked, but Turnbull stayed clamped shut.

"We've got to get him back to town," BG said.

Witherspoon told Lewis to get up behind Abrams, because they were both small, lightweight men, and me and Red boosted Turnbull into Lewis's saddle.

Turnbull groaned at the pain and bit his lips, but he didn't scream out, and once the leg was hanging free, he relaxed some.

Red and I stayed on either side of him in case he fell. It was a little past noon.

At Burleigh's Flat, the sorrel could walk downhill with Lewis on his back.

It was close to midnight by the time we reached Buttonwillow, then when we were trying to decide whether to put Turnbull in Doc's office or in jail, Turnbull spoke up for the first time.

"I'll go to my own house."

None of us cared, we were so tired. While B. G. Hall went for Doc, they let me and Red make a chair out of our hands and carry him inside.

We put him on the sofa in the study, while the others stayed outside waiting for Doc.

Red figured out it was us three alone maybe for the first and last time, and he looked square at Turnbull and asked, "Why?"

Turnbull stared back at him, then me, and said, "You're the only decent ones around here. Why I fired Gibbon? He was hired only to stop the rustling."

"But why run?" Red's voice stayed soft like the way he'd talk to a wild colt.

"My brother is in a hospital in Sacramento. Jean Louise sent a messenger last night. Danny was asking for me . . . Now . . . it's too late . . ."

Terrible things began to add up in my head that I couldn't believe. The blood on the pillow. The unknown rider last night.

"Why the washed carpet, the clothes in the trash?"

"Hot temper, broken heart. A man can be gutted out by a woman . . ." He paused to rest a moment, a sadness settling over his heavy face. "There was a little blood on the carpet from my brother's lungs giving way . . . I suppose the gossips made it sound worse."

Witherspoon and Doc came in, both of them tired, but at least Doc had had some sleep.

He looked at the broken and torn joint, shook his head, and looked directly at Turnbull.

"I can set it straight so you can walk part normal, or I can set it bowed so you can set a saddle. Which way do you want to go?"

Turnbull thought about it, then asked, "If you set it bowed now, can you break it later on and set it straight?"

"Yes, I can do that, but the pain—"

"Set it bowed first, Dr. Meredith," Turnbull said clearly. "There's things to take care of before I can ever walk straight again."

=== 13 ===

T HE NIGHTS TURNED CRISP AND COLD, THE COTTONWOOD
leaves yellowed and blew down to drift away, and it was
coming on time for us to drift on south, too, but we
figured we'd best be square with Buttonwillow before we
left, otherwise somebody would judge we'd abandoned
the ranch and the buildings would start walking off a
board at a time.

Red made a sweet potato pie, layering the sliced
potatoes with molasses, allspice, and cinnamon, then
drenched them with diluted grog before buttoning it all
down with the top crust.

We tried it hot and he said we ought to save a piece for
Mrs. Peyton Cole.

"Who's Mrs. Peyton Cole?"

"The lady that wrote the recipe. It gives all the
directions and said when it was done, to send her a
piece."

"Where did you get the recipe?"

"From a book called *Mrs. Cole's Art of Cookery.*" He
nodded, tasting his own heavenly handiwork.

"When was it printed?"

Looking into a worn, leather-bound volume, he read aloud, "Williamsburg, Virginia, 1837."

"I reckon Mrs. Cole would be past her prime now to enjoy her piece of pie, so why don't we split it in her memory?"

Later on, after Red blew out the lamp, I thought some on Beecher Turnbull and his brother and that pretty memory my mind brought out again, because we were going back into town for the first time since the blowup.

I sure appreciate knowin' you, Wesley . . .

I dream of Jeanie with the light brown hair . . .

We stopped in at Aufdemburg's Mercantile for a supply of raisins and dried currants for the trip south, and the first thing Aufdemburg said was, "I'm glad you're still alive."

It wasn't that he said it—he whispered it and looked over his shoulder.

"Somethin' wrong more'n usual?" I asked.

"She's back . . . staying at Ma Lewis's."

"This damn town don't ever change," I growled. I paid Aufdemburg, and had just turned to follow Red out to the horses when she came in.

Still a handsome woman, she was no longer a pretty girl. A faint haze masked the mischief in her eyes, and a little downward line troubled her smile. Her brown hair was tied up and pinned down in a severe bun.

She came up to me like I was a long-lost friend and took my hand. She tried to look me square in the eyes, but she aimed a trifle low, and when she said, "It's sure good to see you, Wesley," there was a kind of practiced throatiness that I'd heard somewhere before.

I stammered, nodded, shook hands hard, and dodged on around her out the door like a bronco that don't want to be rode, and with Red alongside marched down the empty street to the Prince Albert.

Doc Meredith was sitting at the poker table, along with

Babe Silliman and Ace Dietjen. Down at the end of the bar Fly Swinner, B. G. Hall, and Bolivar Cromwell, all dressed up in their Sunday best, were watching us nervously.

Marvin Bohn looked up when we came to the bar, his flat expression not saying welcome or git, just flat as a paving stone waiting for you to say somethin'.

"A little beer," I said.

The hooded, shoe-button eyes under the derby looked at Red, who shrugged and shook his head.

"Well, thank the Lord of Hosts on high!" BG boomed. "Welcome to this temple, Wesley, Red."

"I'm glad somebody knows me," I said. "We dropped by to say we'd be back come spring."

"I guess you won't miss anythin' here," Bolivar Cromwell said. "I'm thinkin' of movin' my practice to Carson . . ."

"Anything wrong I should know about?" I asked into the quiet gloom.

"Population's fallin' off," Ace Dietjen said, turning over a card.

"We had our second funeral this month just an hour ago," Babe Silliman said. "BG and Fly have struck a bonanza."

"How did you like the way I did the Twenty-third Psalm this morning?" BG asked Babe.

"I thought maybe you put a little more heart into it last week," Babe said.

"Might I inquire as to whom we are missin' from our ranks?" I asked, looking at Marvin Bohn.

"Ask Doc, he's sober," Bohn said.

"Doc?" I turned back to the cardplayers.

"Widow Lewis is now sleeping better knowing her husband is no longer roaming in the night."

I knew right then what I was getting into, but once it's started you can't stop it.

"And then a few days ago, Bud Mabry's horse come in with blood on the saddle," Doc sighed.

"Did you find Bud?" I asked.

"Yesterday Marshal Witherspoon found him facedown by the ashes of a little campfire," Ace Dietjen said. "Next to him was a dead bull calf bearing a fresh Circle M, then right close by was a Tee-Bar cow with her tits a-draggin' on the ground, waitin' to be milked."

"And in the ashes was Mabry's runnin' iron, I suppose?"

"Yes. Looked like Bud took a chance on the spur of the moment," Babe Silliman put in.

"And rode to hell bareback," I said.

"Likely," Ace Dietjen nodded. "But Bud never really rustled for profit. He liked to show how much he hated Beecher Turnbull."

"Either way I guess you'd still have to call it rustlin'," Babe allowed.

Wolf Aufdemburg waddled in and went straight to the other end of the bar, where E. Mickelsen Abrams was waiting in the shadows. They commenced talking in voices too low to hear, but it was pretty plain they weren't just passin' the time of day.

Abrams kept his face turned toward the storekeeper, not wasting any time in giving out his instructions.

Aufdemburg seemed to be trying to say no, but not having much luck, because Abrams was playing his mortgages like they were top trumps. The storekeeper's white, suety face was shining with sweat and his eyes roamed all over the place, fearful as a mustang finding himself in a trap.

Whatever Abrams was saying, Aufdemburg didn't like it, but Abrams was going to have his way, like it or not.

I was some surprised Abrams was still in town the way his friends were dying off. Maybe he thought the flea-bit town would make him a fortune if he could only get around Turnbull. Maybe he knew a secret we didn't know, like a railroad coming over, or a new silver strike, or Lillie Langtry was interested in setting up an opera house. Whatever advantage or smell of profit it was, it held him against plain common sense.

There was just no doubt Turnbull was a dangerous and determined man and very hard to kill.

It was none of our business. I'd finished my beer, glanced at Red, and laid my dime out on the bar when we heard a thump and grinding crossing the boardwalk to the batwing doors. As they opened wide, Turnbull himself came in, with a grotesque gyrating motion. He'd take a step forward with his left leg, shove off with his stiff right leg, and pivot on his left boot heel, then swing the stiff leg around in an arc, plant it, and go through the motion again.

Nodding to Red and me, he went to the middle of the bar where there was no one between him and Abrams.

Abrams shot him a fierce look over his shoulder, and Wolf Aufdemburg seemed to fade away, moving back to the wall, then edging toward the front door.

"I gotta get back to the store . . ." Aufdemburg mumbled, as if he was afraid someone might ask him to stay and have a drink.

"Whiskey," Turnbull said, his eyes fixed on Abrams.

Bohn put a glass and a bottle on the bar in front of him, and Turnbull said, "Pour it for me. I don't trust this banker man enough to turn my back on him."

Bohn poured the glass and put it in Turnbull's open fingers.

"Now let's remember brotherhood and what our Saviour died for," B. G. Hall boomed out, backing away to the other side of Red.

"Shut up," Turnbull said and tossed down the drink.

"What are you afraid of, Turnbull?" Abrams asked in a quiet voice. "We're both businessmen. We both know the rules."

"My knee is calling you a liar," Turnbull said, his right hand close to the butt of his Peacemaker.

"Those are scare words." Abrams made his steel-trap

smile. "I deal only in numbers. Why don't you sell out to me and start enjoying life?"

"I'm enjoying my life," Turnbull said. "Every time one of your partners dies, I laugh my head off."

"You can't get around well enough to manage all your holdings, your wife . . ."

"Is none of your business, Abrams!" Turnbull roared, took a step forward, and slapped the side of Abrams's face with an open left hand that sounded like the crack of a mule skinner's popper.

Abrams's face turned pale and then red.

"I don't carry a gun," he gritted, "but by God I'm going over to the bank and get one."

"You do that, and make out your will, too," Turnbull grinned broadly. "I'll meet you wherever you say."

"In the street," Abrams snapped, then turned abruptly and went out the door.

"You all heard him," Turnbull said, looking around the room. "I've got to defend myself."

There was a murmur of neutral nonsense, with nobody saying that he'd come in looking for a fight and found it.

"Reckon I'd like a piece of Melba's cherry pie," I said to Red, and led the way out to the boardwalk just as E. Mickelsen Abrams went into the bank catty-cornered across the square.

"Funny time to be hungry," Red said as we crossed the street, aiming for Ed's Cafe.

I glanced back over at the mercantile, two doors down from the Prince Albert, and saw Wolf Aufdemburg standing in the doorway, his hands behind his back.

"I thought you was one of them pie fanciers," I said as we reached the front door of the cafe. "But if you are set on backslidin', let's rest here a bit."

Turning to face the town's only intersection, I had a fair view of the saloon on one corner, the bank catty-cornered, and also the harness shop and mercantile just across the street.

I saw Turnbull, big and bulky, standing in the doorway

of the P.A. waiting. I saw Aufdemburg in his doorway telling a couple ladies to get off the street.

There were other men now gathered in safe places, watching the center square, waiting for the dance to commence, like all it needed was for the fiddler to stomp his boot three times and draw his bow.

Abrams stepped out the open bank door with what looked like a .36-caliber Navy Colt on his hip, a weapon light enough for a banker to lift and aim, and stood there waiting.

"Come on out!" he yelled.

Turnbull moved like a big black bull from the shadowed doorway, crabbed his way across the boardwalk, gripped the hitch rail with his left arm, and let himself down into the dusty street.

He paused there, waiting for Abrams to make a move, but Abrams still stood in front of his open door.

"Come on out where I can see you!" Abrams yelled again.

"You too, Mex, you too!" Turnbull boomed. "I don't want any gossips saying it wasn't a fair fight."

Abrams took a slow step forward, and Turnbull took two before he realized Abrams had a plan all of his own.

By then he was a good way out into the square, where everybody in town could see him.

Turnbull stopped, settled himself, and yelled, "No farther!"

Abrams tried to do two things—draw and scuttle back into the bank—at the same time. Likely it was his best move, because he wasn't a gunman and Turnbull was.

His plan almost worked. He just didn't reckon on how fast Turnbull could draw and fire. If he'd dived instead of sidestepping, he might have made it into the bank's safety while Wolf Aufdemburg brought the double-barreled twelve-gauge from behind his back to shoot Turnbull square in the back ribs with a load of double-ought buckshot that tore through his lungs and blasted him forward with arms widespread.

My bullet took Aufdemburg smack in the heart before he could pull the second trigger, but I was still too late.

Abrams lay half in and half out of the bank, kicking spasmodically, and Turnbull managed to roll over on his back, rocking back and forth as the blood burbled out of his mouth, smearing the lower half of his face.

A scattergun makes an oozy corpse, and when I knelt down beside him, neither one of us had any hope.

He stared up at me, knowing full well his life was measured in seconds, and I said, "Any messages?"

"God . . . damn . . . her . . . eyes . . ." he coughed out slowly, one word at a time, and started over again, "God . . . damn . . . her . . ."

The curtain of the long night opened and the light went out of his eyes. He was still rocking back and forth.

Witherspoon was there, and Doc, and then the rest of the townsfolk commenced rambling slowly around from Aufdemburg to Turnbull to Abrams.

"Let's pass on the pie," Red said.

=== 14 ===

Y OU THINK IF I'D ASKED HER TO COME ALONG, SHE WOULD have?" I asked Red.

"She'd do anything to get out of Buttonwillow," Red replied drowsily.

"I appreciate the compliment, but I'm talkin' serious."

"I am too, and the answer is still yes."

"Just because Turnbull didn't want her anymore?"

"And Mex Abrams is dead, and the rest are either too old or too broke."

"You don't rate her too high."

"How many men did she get killed?"

"They weren't all her fault."

"She's young. She's just gettin' started."

"Dang it, I was layin' here kind of dreaming of building a nice house out on the ranch for her and gettin' the family started."

"Likely by now she's been discovered by a politician in Carson and he's already building somethin' fancier."

"You're a hard-hearted injun," I grumbled.

"If she was my wife, I'd cut her nose off, and split her

ears." Red leaned back in his hammock and told Carmelita to keep on fanning with her palm frond.

Alejandra brought me a coconut that she'd topped with a machete and poured in some dark rum and some mashed-up pineapple.

"Más tarde," I said. *"Quiero una cerveza fría, por favor."*

"You're pickin' up the lingo pretty good," Red said. "You don't need no big-eyed palomino mare nickerin' at you."

Our hammocks hung in the shade of a palm grove where the sea breeze kept the mosquitoes away, and the waves down on the beach sloshed in without enthusiasm.

At night we stayed in palm-thatched palapas on higher ground where there was a cool breeze all night and a man could sneak away from all the singing and dancing and get some rest.

I hadn't had my boots on for three months and most times we wore only Levi's chopped off at the knees.

The San Blas folks never got used to my scars, always pointing and giggling, but they weren't afraid and treated us like we were heaven-sent messengers from the north. The poke full of double eagles helped, but it wasn't everything.

I think they were bored with living their lives out on the beach, having the best of food and drink and never having any problems except a hurricane once a year that cleaned off everything.

So when a couple knotheaded buckaroos turned up, they wanted to be nice and help out, for lack of anything more interesting to do.

We taught 'em our language, which was more Texas cowpoke talk than English, but it didn't make any difference to them.

"Light and fill up," I taught Alejandra to say whenever a visitor arrived. Then "Name you pizen," or "I be rumsquaddled!"

They had a lot of laughs learning our language, and

likely they were teachin' us the same damn foolishness. Things like *"Hay moros," "Vale madre," "Besa me mucho," "A la cama,"* such simple things that don't carry no overtones of backshooting and misery.

"Don't you kind of miss shoveling snow from the cabin to the barn every morning?" I murmured, feeling Alejandra's soft fingers on my shoulder, gently rocking the hammock.

"I relish more the hot summers when the only water you can find is alkali," Red replied drowsily.

"Snow'll be gone time we reach the range, and if we don't pick up our colts, somebody else will."

"I never yet did anything smart, Nez," he said agreeably.

"We got to do it."

"Reckon Carmelita and Alejandra would like to try horse ranchin'?"

"Likely not." I shook my head.

"Reckon they'll wait for us to come back?" The sharp little features inside his big face squinched up in silent laughter.

"No," I said, "but their sisters will."

Big Sur Writer

Writing Westerns

by Jim Cole

The Coast Weekly

JACK CURTIS JUST HAD TO WIND UP WRITING WESTERNS. ONE grandfather, his favorite, ran a saloon in a dusty cowboy town in western Kansas and had met Jesse James. Rumor had it he may have shot a man.

"Being an average boy," Curtis said, "I was enamored with this stuff a lot more than with my other grandfather —who was a straight, up-and-coming cattleman." Those extremes—the gunslinging ne'er-do-well and the honest owner of a thousand-acre ranch—produced Curtis.

Most of the year Curtis and his wife, LaVonn, can be found either at their Apple Pie Ranch in Big Sur, or in San Juan Bautista, where he works in a humble two-bedroom house, a photo of his mustachioed and steely-eyed grandfather ("my no-good grandfather," in Curtis's words) watching him. His career—through poetry, short stories, novels, and Hollywood—has gone full circle. Curtis has settled into his Western writing. It's a genre that he never really escaped.

Like so many Midwestern farmers, the Curtis family

was driven from the land in the 1930s. "I'm a Dust Bowler," he said in an interview in San Juan Bautista. "Not exactly the Joad family, but close enough. My father lost everything. I believe he stole the car we drove west in. Loaded it up and took off, and sold our stuff as we came over to buy gas."

In Fresno, his father left him and his mother. Curtis began working to help make ends meet but he knew he wanted to write. He went to Fresno State University, where he edited the campus newspaper and began writing and selling poetry. After a military tour during World War II, he decided to abandon journalism, turning down a job offer at the *Fresno Bee*. "I thought I could affect the world in a positive way more as a fiction writer," he said. So he began to write in earnest, making a living by building houses while LaVonn taught school.

In the late 1940s he struck upon the idea of self-sufficiency, and he and LaVonn staked a claim in the Los Burros Mining District in Big Sur's Los Padres National Forest. "I wanted to see if I could live without taxicabs," he said. Five miles from Highway 1 and without utilities, the two planted orchards, raised chickens, and tried to live off the land.

"The thing is we couldn't. We kept going broke," Curtis said. "I could never get the writing going to make much money at it. But I was a great idealist. I still am." So in the late fifties they moved to Prunedale to build a home and settle down. Christmas Eve, 1960, just shy of completion, their home caught fire and was destroyed. But that wasn't all they lost. "My best novel was burned up in this fire, and I hadn't made copies," he said.

Director Sam Peckinpah, a high school friend, came to his rescue, offering him a job as a Hollywood scriptwriter. He caught on fast and soon was working on his own, selling his services to the highest bidder. For twelve years he worked for Hollywood writing for a batch of popular shows, including *Have Gun Will Travel, Wagon Train,*

The Rifleman, and *Zane Grey Theater.* In addition, he wrote for *Dr. Kildare, The Corruptors,* and *Ben Casey.*

Jack and LaVonn built another place in Big Sur. Their Apple Pie Ranch has electricity and phone service, so he could work for Hollywood from there. But twelve years of Hollywood was plenty. "I was fifty years old and I was worn out," he said. "I was tired. I was just finished with it."

Ten years later he was off on another adventure, building a house in Mexico. Every October he takes his typewriter and research books and moves to Baja California, where he can write from sunrise to sundown.

Six years ago an agent asked him if he had any Westerns. His response was not surprising. "I'm a natural Western writer."

With one and a half Westerns, *The Sheriff Kill* and *Texas Rules,* already done, Curtis began examining what was on the market. He was not impressed. "Gee whiz," he thought at the time, "Westerns are really going downhill, or I've changed."

And he told himself, "I think there's an opportunity here for a good writer, in all modesty."

"I want to get the writing, I want to get the poetry, I want to get the humor, I want to get the music," he said. "I don't want to be one-dimensional; I want to be three-dimensional."

Curtis has become a stickler for accuracy, researching dates and historic events, studying guns and inventories from nineteenth-century general stores. Last year, he and LaVonn returned to the Midwest and drove from Texas to Montana following the trail of the last cattle drive as part of his research for his most ambitious Western, *Purple Iris.*

On a shelf in his San Juan Bautista study he has the *Book of Inventory of Beeman & Co.,* from an 1892 general store in San Francisco. He flipped through the pages and read about hairpins, Indian muslin, cocaine for 84 cents, Jamaica Ginger (used in bootleg whiskey), hay rakes, bridle bits, cartridges, and a revolver for $5.20.

On another shelf he has a replica of an 1860 Army Colt .44 revolver made by his son. There is also a collection of books—the *University of Chicago Spanish Dictionary* beside the Bible, *Cowboy Slang, The Best of the American Cowboy,* and an *1897 Century Atlas of the World*—that shows western Nebraska empty, western South Dakota nothing.

And above the books is a century-old photo of a mustachioed fellow wearing a wide necktie and a jacket. He has the steely gaze of a man who could very well have shot somebody and who will watch over his grandson as he tries to write about it a century later.

The *only* authorized biography of the legendary man who inspired two of the year's biggest movie events!

WYATT ☆ EARP
FRONTIER MARSHAL

"No man could have a more loyal friend than Wyatt Earp might be, nor a more dangerous enemy."
— Bat Masterson

"Earp never hunted trouble, but he was ready for any that came his way." —Jimmy Cairns, deputy marshal, Wichita, Kansas

"I am not ashamed of anything I ever did." — Wyatt Earp